T0276642

Praise for Jo

"Alfred Jarry on speed? Yes, but better!"

**— Michael T. Cisco, author of *Pest*
and *Antisocieties***

"Jose Elvin Bueno is not just an intelligent writer but
a creator of one of the most energetic fiction styles out
there. His books contain a propulsiveness that makes
reading enjoyable."

**— Eileen Tabios, author of *The
Balikbayan Artist* and *DoveLion: A
Fairy Tale for our Times***

"*Subversivo, Inc.* takes place in an alternate Philippines populated by an outstanding cast of characters
reflecting current observations of the Filipino condition, deftly juggling themes of power, political
inequality, the impact of technology, and games
people play in a narrative dense with telling details.
The modern and the mundane stand side by side with
the marvelous, intertwining different strands of story.
A thoroughly engaging book that offers much food for
thought."

**— Dean Francis Alfar, author of
Salamanca (A Novel), *The Kite of
Stars and Other Stories*,**

GIGANTVM PENISIVM

A Tale of Demonic Possession

Jose Elvin Bueno

HORROR

Copyright © 2024 by Jose Elvin Bueno

Cover by Matthew Revert

ISBN: 9781960988348

CLASH Books

Troy, NY

This one's for the couples:

Tricia and Paul
Portia and Sunny
Rica and JC

GIGANTVM PENISIVM

PROLOGUE

Never listen to the silence in your head.
Ever.
That void in between your ears? Avoid it at all cost.

Fill it up with shit. There's porn. There's drugs and alcohol. There's even, if you are really desperate, social fucking media.

One listen, that's all it takes, and you're done.

One listen and you'll see your true self.

Never listen to the silence in your head.

I have this silence in my head.

This void.

This emptiness that is driving me mad.

No, I do not fear it.

I just want it to go away. To leave me in peace and stop bothering me.

To stop me from thinking about me. The real me.

The me me.

I have this silence in my head.

Chapter One

This is a story about what is happening this Friday. Think of what I am telling you as a novel. And just like any other novel, our story has characters. One would be me and the rest are my friends whom I will introduce in a few.

We also have a setting. This will also be revealed soon.

And of course, we have conflicts and complications.

And for an ending, we will have an explosive climax.

Let me say it again: an explosive climax.

In other words, shit will happen in our story. Oh yes, shit will definitely happen.

But our story is very different from all the others that have ever been told.

Why?

Because our story does not have a lesson.

Trust me on this. Please. You will learn nothing. Not a single thing.

Also, if happy endings happen to be your shit, now would be a good time to leave. Go snap a selfie for your Insta. Troll that fucker on FB. Do that latest craze on TikTok. Just go.

With that out of the way, let us begin.

Our novel starts with how every story starts.

With optimism.

Friday is like the New Year of the week. Or is that the New Day of the week? Calendars tell us that the week begins on a Sunday, or if you are a corporate monkey, that would be on a Monday. But the week really begins on a Friday.

Because everything is possible on a Friday.

Every fucking thing.

You can do whatever you want on a Friday.

You can do whoever you want on a Friday.

You can be whoever you want on a Friday.

Friday is permissive, Friday is non-judgmental, Friday is an enabler. If you want to try something you haven't done before, do it on a Friday. If you want to ask a huge favor from someone, say something involving money in the millions of pesos, do it on a Friday. If you want to fuck your best friend's girlfriend or boyfriend, the best chance of being able to score is, yes, on a Friday.

We all know this, don't we?

Mondays to Thursdays are your parents, Fridays are your friends. Mondays to Thursdays are the spreadsheets, Fridays are the selfies. Mondays to Thursdays are the saints and the angels, Fridays are the sluts and the devils.

Mondays to Thursdays are inconsequential, boring, suicidal. Fridays? Fridays are cool, awesome, alive!

Okay, a few examples. Be fucking honest with me now.

Who among us had to submit a corporate report on a Friday? How did it turn out? Took an exam on a Friday and aced it? Broke up with your BAE on a Friday and was happy about it?

See? You don't give a shit about these things on a Friday, because Friday itself does not give a shit.

Ever heard the term "I can't even...?" Yes, Friday invented that.

And did I tell you that you can be whoever you want on a Friday?

Now let's circle back to when this shit started.

It is a Friday as I have already said.

I am at home. I am at home shredding some stupid resignation letter that I did not hand over to my stupid boss because, what else, it is a fucking Friday and I couldn't be bothered. Who resigns on a Friday? Anyway, I have just taken off my tie, one of the reasons I wanted to quit my stupid job in the first place and was staring at a very cold beer inside the fridge when I get an iMessage.

From Basti.

"Rafa! Let's do something different. My place at nine. Everyone's going to be here. Don't wear your Grandpa's aftershave."

Yes, I have to explain that message if we have to continue with our story.

Chapter Two

Hello! Have I got a story for you, my lurves.

Yep, a story.

A real story that's as awesome as this Friday.

Now, think of what I am telling you as a series of scheduled Instagram posts. A clickable story experience with multi-panel stories. A real story!

Filled with beautiful people, including moi, of course. All are friends, all are followers, all are @mention.

There is a location. And as per yoozh, it is 'grammable AF. Because, brand aesthetic. This place is real, it's neither staged nor 'shopped. You'll see how awesome it is. Soon. But, to protect both the innocent and the guilty, it will not be geotagged. Nope, not even a location sticker. Sorry, not sorry.

I will be doing the words—think of them as captions—in real time as things begin to happen. Awesome words that will tease you, my lurves, and leave you aching for more.

Now, my story is different from all the other stories that have ever been published and shared and hearted on Insta.

Why?

Because my story has a lesson.

I know you trust me on this, my lurves.

There is a moral to be had. Yep, there is a moral!

Because why else would I tell you a story, my lurves, if you will learn nothing?

As I begin my story, all I ask from you is to look beyond the filter, forget that an edit is taking place before it is posted, and ignore the fact that there is a content creation workflow being followed to make it even more engaging.

Think of this request as an end-user agreement. Oui?

With that out of the way, it's time to click here and view more.

Let me preface my story by saying that I live for Fridays.

Friday is the one day in the week when things really happen. When I make things really happen. When I am alive, when I am in control, when I am me.

Allow me to explain how my week goes, my lurves.

Monday. This should be declared and observed as Sunday 2 point o. When I get to sleep 'til 3 in the afternoon or just lounge around in the pool. Basically, rehydration time. But no. What really happens is that I restart my week and put it on overdrive. There are models and film stars who need to be styled and this could either be a shoot or a pre-prod. And I have to be on my A game. As for my socials, all are scheduled AF. FB is the first to fire off, by around 10 in the AM and this awesomeness is bounced around Twitter, TikTok, Snapchat, the works. My vlog entry soon follows by around 12 noon. A scheduled post on Insta is released into the wild by 3 PM. These times are not randomly selected but are the results of analytics and algorithms. Anals and algos, everything internet revolves around these two. I post when my fans and followers are most likely to engage. Of course, I make an exception when there is an occasion. New Year's for example, deserves a midnight post. If an A List celebrity dies or an international tragedy occurs, it is best to publish something within the next 5 minutes, but only if these are worthy of newsjacking. If a brand is paying me enough moolah to peddle a product, a post will be pushed at an agreed-upon time. But only for enough moolah. And only in US dollars. As this is Monday, there will be no new content on my OnlyFans but a dope teaser will be posted. And this teaser will have a shorter version on my PornHub. Tuesday to Thursday. I am in the flow. Still doing either film or photo shoots. Or, if schedule permits, one, just one, pre-prod tucked sometime in the day. Let me take you through the shoots. Mostly these are commercial shoots. For TV ads or vids that end up as social media content of brands and businesses. I dress talents according to the vision of the director. This is the easy part. The hard part is convincing the director first, and then the client second, why the talent or talents should be dressed the way I see it. Another hard part is sourcing the dress, because if worse comes to worst, I will have to make the dress myself. A photo shoot is just the still version of the film shoot but instead of a director, I deal with a photographer. A real photographer and not some noob with an iPhone and a fucking ring light. Frankly, I prefer photo shoots, especially photo shoots where the client is a fashion brand, but film shoots pay a whole lot more and tend to land more projects, especially if the director considers me a part of his or her crew. As for the pre-prod, it is basically a face-to-face where I present my idea, then the look, and finally the cost. This means getting my aesthetics sold and sold well. I get a contract signed by the client and the director or photog. And, equally important, a check auto-graphed by whoever is holding the moneybag. As for my socials, these days are no different from a Monday, all go off at the preset time. While on smoking breaks, I snap photos and write down words and make notes for future posts. Mostly about ideas for my OnlyFans. I never peek behind the curtain and look at the numbers. Ever. Now is not the time for KPI. Or—l'horreur!—ROI. I don't want to stress myself any more than I have to by worrying about the hearts and the dollars, the views and the shares, not to mention the comments and the requests

or, fuck them all, the bashers and the trolls. After hours, if it is
not too late, are for drinks with friends. After after hours are for
creating content, editing it, and psyching myself up for the
filming of my next OnlyFans vid.

So, basically, Mondays to Thursdays are more of the same
and same of the more.

Et voila! Friday!

But first, le weekend.

Saturday. It depends on how wild the day before was. And
if there are any spillover shoots. And if Gio and 'Gette, AKA
The Fam, want to see me. If I have the day to myself, half of
that goes to sifting through the brands that want me as their
brand ambassador because they all think that I am an—fuck
this word—influencer. The rest of the day goes to perfecting the
filters of my shots and my vids, doing the edits and the layers
and the soundtrack, and writing down a draft and rewriting
that very same draft for my vlog. I do myself for the next Only-
Fans drop and polish that, too. Then everything is calendared
for calibrated posting. I treat myself to a large fry and Coke
from Mickey D's. And then I look at the numbers. Relevance
scores, conversion rates, average response times, reach, traffic,
the works. Numbers don't lie. And not only do numbers not lie,
they also answer two existential questions. One. Do people still
give a shit? Two. Do they still pay as if they give a shit? After
the digits have been noted and the moolah accounted for, I
meet my friends for a drink or two. I supply the snow.

Sunday. Rehydration time as I have already said. A one-
person pajama party in my bed if I am really hammered or a
one-person pool party in the backyard if I feel like it. Zero
social media. As in I do not even look at my phone. Rehydration time, remember? I have to detox myself from all the toxic
shit that is in there. And just how do I do that, my lurves? One.
A physical calendar where I pencil in all that will be
happening in the upcoming week. Two. Voicemail service.
Those that dare call me on a weekend about work know that

they need to leave a message and that I will only reply by around Monday noon. At the earliest.

Now, Friday.

Fridaaaaaaaaaaaaayyy!!!

Fridaaaaaaaaaaaaayyy!!!

Friday, while still a workday, is actually my day. My me day. It's all about moi.

This means that on a Friday, I get to totally decide everything.

When it comes to projects, I only take the ones whose talents I really want to style.

When it comes to brands, I only push those that I really lurve.

And when it comes to friends, I only meet those whom I really want to meet. And only after hours of course, when the director or the photog has called it a day.

Let nobody tell you, my lurves, that I am not a pro.

Now on this particular Friday in my story, I decide to meet @Basti.

Chapter Three

First, Basti.

He is my friend. We grew up together, went to school together, got circumcised together, fell in love with the same girls together, had our first blowjobs from the same girl together, got our first jobs in the same firm together.

Okay, that's not true. About the job.

I still have a job, at least for now, while Basti, well, he is into the family business since day one like a lot of our friends. More on that later.

Anyway, we are practically brothers.

I spent a lot of Fridays with him. And this particular Friday would not be different from the rest. We will hang out, I will tell him about my aborted resignation, he will tell me that it was a very bad decision to chicken out quitting your job even on a Friday, and we will laugh about it and get high.

———————

Next, "Rafa."

Rafa is me.

Rafa is short for Rafael Gutierrez.

You always know that an iMessage—even a group one—comes from Basti because he announces whom he wants to talk to, as if he shouting to a huge crowd. Same when calling, too, with his calls always starting with "Rafa, it's me Basti" as if iPhones do not have a caller ID. As if he needs to validate his very being by calling out his name.

As if without his name, he is nothing.

Next, "Let's do something different."

About this, I honestly do not have a clue.

Because to Basti, different is different. Different is drinking bootleg moonshine inside a dimly lit speakeasy. In Williamsburg, Brooklyn. Twelve years ago, when he was two years under the legal drinking age.

That kind of different.

Or hiring the midget wrestlers and drag queens from that expat bar in Willamsburgos, Makati to perform a gladiator combat sport and a Lady Gaga retrospective complete with that meat dress. Don't laugh, it really happened.

Now, it could be a recruitment for some pyramid scam via a PowerPoint presentation involving designer nutrition supplements just for the hell of it. *Open-minded ka ba?*

You've guessed it right. Basti is not a scenester.

He is the scene.

I have no idea what to expect, which, I think, is part of what makes this Friday, a Friday.

Next, "Everyone's going to be here."

It means that the usual suspects will be there at his crib.

Mitzi. Pia. Vicente. And Basti himself, of course.

As for the aftershave, it's just a stupid joke so let's not get into that.

And so, I go.

But only because today is a Friday.

Chapter Four

Friday.

My me day.

I am in a film shoot with a Hollywood has-been who's in Manila to be a brand ambassador of an international chain of hotels and casinos because she is an—*fuck this word*—influencer. Now, I have already mentioned that the only projects that I take on a Friday are the ones I really want.

This is one of those projects. Because of this has-been. To be more precise, because of the has-been's contract. To be even more precise, because of the rider in that contract.

Allow me to explain, my lurves.

All talents have contracts, the papers with signatures on them basically detailing what is going to be exchanged and for how much. What the talent will do for what amount of cash. Most of these contracts are as standard as they come as these are cooked up by law firms, seasoned by insurance companies, and served by talent agencies.

Now, contracts get interesting whenever a talent is hot AF. And I don't mean in bed but in market value.

At this point in my story, I am spilling one of the secrets of the biz: one's market value is directly proportional to one's *hotness in bed. Example? Moi! See, my lurves? I can also do modesty.*

But don't let me distract you with my awesomeness.

Anyhoo.

Once a talent is considered hot enough, he or she, gets to demand shit that is outside of the signed contract. This demand is called a rider. Say, a celebrity wants a Moët chilled to a specified temperature waiting for her in the dressing room.

Now let's go back to this particular Friday in my story.

As I have already said, the reason I took this project is the has-been's rider.

And the rider is this: a bunch of white chrysanthemums.

In the biz, the words "white chrysanthemums" do not mean the flower but cocaine. What I call as snow. The code words used to be "baby powder" but an incident occurred that almost made it to the press involving a, you guessed it, real baby powder brand, so everyone in the industry settled on the flower. Simple enough to understand, and not too obvs as to be vulgar.

Whenever white chrysanthemums appear in the rider, this means that what's really happening is a partaaaaaaaaaaaaayyy!!! With just a film shoot on the side.

I check the contract and there it is in black and white, the has-been has requested this particular flower and has an entourage of seven people with every single one having an All-Access designation, confidentiality of the ad campaign be damned.

Now, when a Hollywood has-been demands a hundred grams of snow, suppliers are wise enough to multiply it by a hundredfold. Maybe more. Being high on the set is what makes the project grind faster, as long as the talent is also a pro, of course.

So, this is how my story starts. A Friday that's basically just a party inside a casino with a chance of snow. And let's not *forget, I get paid, too. In cold hard cash as what I always demand when I take on these kinds of shoots.*

———————

By the time everyone on the set is high as a kite and the filming has moved on to shooting B rolls and safety shots, I get an iMessage from @Basti, asking if he can call me.

As @Basti is more of an iMessage dude, I make a guess that something must be up if he wants a voice call.

I take five and head out of the casino floor to one of the hotel suites that I am using as a dressing room. I flash my laminate to the hired muscle by the door as my iPhone rings.

"Mitzi, it's me, Basti."

You know @Basti, right, my lurves? This is how he opens his calls. Always introducing himself like a co-conspirator about to commit a crime

"Ça va?" I reply.

"Listen. I'm doing something fun tonight."

"Sure, you are."

"Seriously, Pia and Vicente will be here. You should definitely come."

"I'm still wrapping up a shoot."

"No worries. Just be sure to beat the storm. I hear this one's a fucker. My place at around nine."

"I can't commit to that time, so don't wait up."

"Just get your awesomeness over here."

With this, @Basti ends the call.

And that's @Basti, my lurves, one of the characters in my story.

Now, are you excited about the setting?

Chapter Five

L et's get the setting out of the way.
Our novel is set in the present year, the current month, and on this week. And as I have already noted, it occurs on a Friday.

As for the place, we are in the Philippines. If you are asking me, this is the greatest country in the world. Really. We have everything here. Like cronuts and baked maki. We also have everyone here. Like stay-in drivers and uniformed maids. See?

If we zoom in a bit, we are in Makati City. Arguably the most modern and moneyed of all the cities in this paradise of seven thousand plus islands.

Like the day that is Friday, Makati is a city of possibilities. Everything is possible here. I have heard stories from my Lolo that this city of high rises and intelligent buildings were rat-ridden rice fields once, if not for the bastard sons of Spanish conquistadores masquerading as Catholic priests who trans-formed it into what it is today. A glistening empire of steel and glass generating untold money and the unlimited privilege that comes with it.

I am inclined to believe my Lolo for I know that he knows

a thing or two about bastard sons. And Catholic priests. More on that later.

To continue.

We are in Makati. If we zoom in a little bit more, we are in one of the inner streets of Salcedo Village. Well-lit by halogen lamps. Neon signs advertising wealth management firms and fast-food outlets. Reflectorized signages declaring surveillance cameras operating 24/7. Manicured greens separating the sidewalks from the pavement and well-maintained shrubs neatly hiding electrified iron fences.

A village, indeed.

And then we go to the weather.

It is a dark and stormy night.

I know! I should have started our story with this killer line, but fuck it.

There is a storm coming, expected to make landfall by around midnight. Typhoon Gerardo or maybe Geronimo, I am not really sure, is packing wind at about 270 kilometers per hour and the whole of Metro Manila is already under storm signal number 3. As strong as Haiyan, according to the office chatter.

Although it was cloudy the entire afternoon, the temperature is hovering at around 33 degrees Celsius. Humidity like breathing water. The city is an oven and we are being preheated on its concrete baking pan. It is hot as fucking hell.

I almost made the coming storm an excuse not to go Basti's.

As I have said, when the iMessage came, I'd already taken off my tie, about to shred my resignation letter, and was staring at the bottles of cold beer inside the fridge. I keep the fridge door open for a couple of minutes letting the cool air waft over me and erase the inferno that I have brought inside my dig.

I know that it would be a cool Friday night just chilling with my beer, watching some dumbass film on Netflix. Something with lots of big guns and fiery explosions. With a Hollywood babe exposing her gigantic, beautiful boobies.

Also, this being a Friday night and with the storm coming, I have already dismissed my driver. Basti's crib is just three blocks away, but still.

Then again, that iMessage. From Basti. Promising that we will be doing something different. Maybe it will have something to do with the storm, who the fuck knows?

And so, of course...

I shed off my long sleeves, dress pants, leather shoes and put on a black crewneck tee, faded Levi's, and my trusted pair of Nikes. My usual Friday night threads. Grabbing a black linen blazer, a-just-in case, I head out.

While it is not yet raining, the clouds are low and black and I could feel that they are angry as fuck. Murderous is the word. Carnivorous is another.

The heat did not retreat and I need to decide whether to hurry up so I can find solace inside Basti's crib the soonest or pace myself so as to not sweat a river.

I take my time walking, the blazer rolled up in one hand.

Except for the approaching storm, it is a typical Friday night.

Bumper-to-bumper traffic of my fellow corporate zombies escaping the city after surviving another grueling work week. Call center boys and girls walking to the night shift, lanyards swaying from their necks. A group of illegal Chinese POGO fuckers smoking by a corner in flagrant violation of a city ordinance. Three maids in uniforms picking up dogshit from three leashed Shih Tzus. There are even a couple of Caucasians filming some stupid crap on a handheld tripod fully loaded with a circular flash attachment and a phallic mic outside a noisy bar. Fucking influencers.

The camera pans and points in my direction. The one speaking to the camera waves at me. I give him the one-finger salute.

I walk on until I see about a dozen men in all-black fatigues with tops in three folds and pants tucked inside tactical boots. Mirrored shades despite the hour. Discreet comms.

The hardware of these badass motherfuckers is admirable, too. Side arms of Desert Eagle 357 Magnum. And big swinging dicks of ArmaLite M16. Like my father, I know a thing or two about guns and other analog killing machines. More on that later.

I salute Basti's private army masquerading as the residential towers' security guards and head to the entrance of his apartment building.

The AC is a huge relief. It bordered on the surreal. Like entering another world. The reality outside vanishes away inside this steel and glass enclave pumped full of manufactured arctic breeze.

A cold beer would make my day and kickstart this Friday. Fucking Basti, this night better be wild.

I high-five the three doormen all rushing to push the button of a private elevator. One even produced a padded hanger and offered to carry my blazer. I wave them all away and head up to the penthouse.

Of course, Basti lives in the penthouse. I'm sure you've guessed that already.

But you will never ever guess the shit that will happen in our story.

Chapter Six

T his is what happens next in my story: back at the casino floor, I hear the director shout the magic words.

"It's a wrap!"

I undress the has-been, catalog the dresses, turn them over to one of the PAs, and have her sign a receipt. The PA, in turn, has me sign a non-disclosure before handing over the moolah for today's work. I count the greenbacks, these blue Benjamins that smell of imperialism at its finest, and pocket them before signing the acknowledgment. Yes, this is one of those projects that I demanded to be paid in cold hard cash.

I say goodbye to the has-been who orders one of the hangers-on to snap a photo of us using her phone. I pose and preen while she vapes and vogues at the camera for a couple of shots. When the has-been asks whether I want a shot on my phone, I politely say yes and snap a selfie. Word travels faster than a meme in the biz and it is best to behave like a pro. Even if it means playing the diehard fan.

Again, let me tell you one of the secrets of the biz: never ask for a selfie from a celeb, even if he or she is a has-been, unless it's *the talent asking for it. And in the event that he or she indeed asks for it, never decline. And lastly and just as important, if you are lucky enough to be granted a selfie using your phone, make sure the talent approves the shot before you save it. Always.*

Anyhoo.

After I have her OK the snap, I say my thanks and sling an air kiss on both her cheeks. I then hand her a Sharpie and have her autograph the mini storyboard printed on the back of my All Access pass and she obliges. I say my thanks again.

The director offers me a beer, a chilled as fuck Kronenbourg 1664 and I take it. I light a Marl red and hand it to him after a long puff. We clink our glasses and stare at the now emptying set. The day is looking like a proper Friday.

We do small talk as we sip our beers and share the smokes. Upcoming projects on the horizon, bitchy clients, and vacation plans. The yoozh.

Another PA walks by and hands me a swag from the casino. The paper bag is big but discreetly branded. But still, a swag. I decline. The signed laminate is good enough for me. Besides, nothing screams has-been more than a swag. It's the beauty queen that gets the bling while the "thank you ladies" take home a bag. So, here is another piece of free advice my lurves: never take home a swag. No matter how tempting. Ever. It is simply not dope.

After we finish our bottles, I say my goodbye to the director. No air kisses, just a high five. Not only am I one of the crew, I am also one of the boys.

He hands me my cut of the white chrysanthemums.

Officially, my day is now a Friday.

And so, with a smile on my face and snow in my bag, I head over to @Basti's.

Think of a filter, my lurves. Specifically, think of the VSCO S2 filter. Et voila! *That's how the setting of my story looks. Clean, bright, modern. On brand. Awesomeness.*

But before I achieve that look, I still have to suffer the weather. The gloomy weather with the clouds hanging so low that, for a second, makes me doubt if going to @Basti is a good idea.

And for a Friday night with an impending storm, the humidity is something. It is alive and aggressive. I feel it assault me the moment I step out of the casino and enter the van provided by the production house. An hour of stewing in traffic and the humidity gets even worse when I finally reach the high rise that houses @Basti. You've all seen my snaps. I dress for the weather but even in my tee shirt and jeans, it is still muggy as fuck.

I sprint from the van to the building's main entrance.

@Basti runs a tight crew and as per yoozh, the doormen scramble to open swing doors and push elevator buttons. They are well mannered too, calling me either Miss Mitzi or Mademoiselle Ricafort complete with a slight bow.

The elevator takes me to the penthouse.

Chapter Seven

At the penthouse, I am the first to arrive. As per yoozh.

"Men..." says Basti as he opens the door of his crib.

That's how he greets people.

"Men..." You can practically hear the ellipsis. As if he wants to say, "Men, what took you so long?" Or, "Men, you would not fucking believe this!" Or, "Men, is everything all right?"

Yes, I know. I am just one person and it should be "Man..." but who gives a shit?

I enter and greet him with mine.

"Sebastian Montes."

I say his name the way I heard it from our homeroom adviser in Grade 1 years ago. The day I learned that he, like me, has a full name. You know, like a real person. Basti is Sebastian Montes.

As Basti leads me into the foyer, I stop him.

"You still haven't accepted my request on Insta," I say.

"Men..." Basti says. "Social media is dead as fuck. Why would you even want to flirt with Insta? You want a dick pic? I have a few if you're at peace with your inner gay."

Basti is a natural comedian so I leave it at that.

———————

Allow me to describe Basti's crib.

It is so bright and so white that it hurts the eyes. I shit you not. It really hurts.

A fucking visual assault that hammers your brain with fucking whiteness. Like a double-spread ad on the latest ish of Wallpaper. Or maybe Monocle. But with some art director going bonkers on Photoshop and saturating the whole shit with whiteness. The whole crib borders on being blinding. Brilliance as a color scheme. White as fucking white for its theme.

The living room is framed by a floor-to-ceiling glass window that ends in a skylight spanning half the ceiling area. Because his unit is at the penthouse, it overlooks the Central Business District with its shopping malls, office buildings, and other residential condominiums. Basti's crib towers over the place. It lords over the land.

A white modular sofa, a Minotti, I still remember what Basti has called it, is the centerpiece. And when I say centerpiece, I mean it sits right there in the center of the cavernous living room and not a single part of this white furniture touches a wall. How sick is that?

Opposite this sofa is a white coffee table surrounded by egg chairs, white of course.

An arc lamp stands by the left of the sofa and its light falls squarely on the low table. Yep, the lamp is bone white.

Ah, the minibar. It is to the right of the sofa with three barstools, a white granite counter housing a small sink, a wine fridge, a liquor cabinet, and another fridge for beer and other bottled drinks.

Behind the bar is a white display shelf that houses Voltes
V robots, Bear Bricks, Star Wars characters, and Bruce Lee
figurines. All collector items and in fucking white.

This wall shelf ends in a white bedroom wall adorned
with posters: *No Sleep Till Brooklyn. I Listen to Bands That
Don't Exist Yet. Helvetica.* Yes, black fonts on white paper
inside white frames.

On a corner sits a record cabinet holding yet more
precious collectibles. First pressing of seventies rock albums
arranged alphabetically. Black Sabbath, Led Zeppelin, Pink
Floyd. The usual crap. Basti believes the human race should
have stopped attempting to make music after 1979 and then
have it restarted by 2019 with the likes of Deafheaven, Salem,
and The Mountain Goats doing the reboot. And that the
format of recording and distribution and appreciation of
anything musical should have not been evolved from the
vinyl.

What a fucking hipster, amirite?

And on top of this white vinyl cabinet is the AKAI
turntable that I helped Basti hunt down in back alleys of
Tokyo.

That the AKAI is not playing any tunes is what makes me
notice the silence.

It is weird.

It is beyond weird.

It is beyond *beyond.*

Another thing I notice is that there is not a single alcoholic
drink anywhere. *Que horror!* Not on the center table, not at
the bar, not in Basti's hand. Usually, Basti will have an opened
bottle of beer ready for me as soon as I enter his place and he
would be finishing his.

"Basti," I say. "This is not an intervention, right? I am not
yet a full-blown alcoholic. Give me a few more years."

"Nothing could be farther from an intervention than this," Basti says. He laughs and adds, "Besides, I swore that we would go to rehab together when the time comes, didn't I? We'll fly to Europe, watch every game of the Champions League live from the quarterfinals to the championship and say we are studying Art History as we purge ourselves clean."

This makes me laugh. That's Basti for you. One smart-mouthed motherfucker.

Although deep inside, I am hoping that the lack of alcohol is just a joke. You know what they say, right? A party without alcohol is just a fucking meeting.

Plus, this is Basti after all. An expert in finding off-the-wall digs and making shit happen. Maybe we'll brave the approaching storm and go out to some hidden bar. Just maybe.

I see that Basti is wearing his usual threads for a Friday night too, so there might still be hope. His I-am-in-the-family-business attire. Ankle-length dark gray work pants and a banker's shirt with subtle stripes. Both are freshly ironed. The long sleeves buttoned all the way to the top like some fucking Brooklynite.

And leather shoes as matte as his longish hair that is slicked back by an industrial strength styling clay to keep the edges from flying away.

Basti is one good looking fucker. Like Ryan Gosling circa *Crazy Stupid Love*. Even that *Blade Runner* sequel. But with an Asian look. Really. Okay, he's really fucking *tisoy*, so there. A friendly kind of face that tapers down to a strong chin. Cute small ears in a girly kind of way. Mount Everest nose. In contrast are his eyes. Under strong brows are deep eyes, that, depending on his mood, either looks disturbing or disturbed.

But back to his Friday night get up before you fuckers think I am in love with this dude.

Basti is in business attire because he is in the family business.

If you are in a family business, you know this. You can dress corporate and mean it ironically.

Did I use that word right? "Ironically?"

And then the doorbell dings.

Chapter Eight

I buzz the door and @Basti—the devil himself, Friday in the flesh—opens it.

And this devil looks slick AF this Friday night in his weekend garb as if he is on the way to a hostile takeover of one of his daddy's companies. The theme is classic corporate. One glance and I could tell he's wearing this season's Paul Smith. And I mean his shirt. The pants, oops, trousers, are Savile Row. His kicks are a pair from Le Marche. Black, leather, oxfords. Très chic. He couldn't have looked any more awesome even if I had styled him myself. And that hair!

Well, my lurves, you know @Basti, right?

If you follow me on Insta, I'm sure you also follow him on his socials. Maybe even stalk him IRL. He's got a few obsessed fans and I don't blame them. Especially the ladies.

And here's the deal with @Basti.

He's one of us, ladies.

Now, before you all jump from the top of buildings or slice your wrists with that steak knife or swallow a gallon of rat poison, allow me to explain.

No, my lurves, he is not a closeted member of La Fédération. No, really, he is not. Swear to gods.

What I mean is that @Basti is a dude who is also a dudette in the sense that he makes those who have the hots for him wait a while. A very long while. The more desperate they are, the more he makes them suffer. He's totes adorbs, this silly little heartbreaker. He can do this because he knows that there is a robust supply chain of willing BAEs waiting for him straight out of the trophy wife factory. His motto is: So Many Fucks to be Had, So Little Time. *This is not a joke, my lurves. He's even got his play towels monogrammed with his initials and embroidered with these very same words in Latin. And in the event that the unthinkable happens and the BAEs dry out, well, he can always buy himself a perfect wife and place her inside a gilded cage, like one of his Bear Bricks in his toy display shelf. This while buying a couple of mistresses, too.*

And you guessed it right, my lurves, this is also true with his friends. How he can buy anyone to be his friend, I mean.

@Basti kisses me by the door.

A real kiss on the lips with just the right amount of tongue.

Now, don't get too excited, my lurves. @Basti is a very close friend and this is how we roll. What's a Frenchie between friends?

Plus, @Basti already has a BAE, @Pia, who is not just a friend but one of the coolest peeps ever.

Although as he kisses me by the door, I have to fess up, my lurves, I get a little moist. To distract myself, I ask him where @Pia is and I learn that she is already on her way. Well.

@Basti leads me inside the penthouse, and as per yoozh, it is screenshottable AF. Sharable. Heartable.

What did I tell you about the setting in my story?

Now, remember that we are in Manila, the greatest city in the world in the sense that not only is inherited wealth not frowned upon, it is also envied. The good news is that when it comes to Basti, all he inherited is wealth and not the tacky taste of his parents with their Amorsolo portraits, the paintings that are the centerpiece of their ancestral home, and what they proudly call pictures as termed by Sotheby's.

But back to Basti's place.

It's like seeing the penthouse through the lens of Insta and having a permanent filter pulled right in front of your very eyes. His crib is so cool. Everything is esthetically pleasing and visually pleasurable. It could be how white everything is. Or how clean the place looks.

Or, it could just be the presence of @Basti himself.

As I head to the living room, I see a ghost.

@Rafa.

Or to be precise, it is now just Rafa.

Chapter Nine

It is Mitzi.

Okay, I have to explain this a bit.

Mitzi is a girl. Beautiful and sexy as fuck.

But she is also a dude.

No. It's not what you think. Really, it's not.

What I mean is, Mitzi is one of those hot girls who is more dude than most dudes.

Like, when it comes to drinking, we are mere mortals before her. Or this. Mitzi wears the same kind of clothes every single day. Black t-shirt and a pair of faded men's straight-cut jeans. Very dirty sneakers. Vans or Chucks that are literally falling to pieces.

Did I use that word right? "Literally?"

I ask because I always hear Pia, whom I will introduce in a few, say, "Ohhheeemgeee, my head literally exploded!"

But it sounds about right every single time Pia says it, "my head literally exploded" so I don't honestly know what's fucking right anymore.

To continue. Mitzi's dude clothes and very dirty shoes. She says that she can get away with it because she is a fashion stylist. Don't ask.

But what makes Mitzi a dude more than you and me, is that she is willing to do anything at least once. Anything at all. So maybe that's why she couldn't resist dropping by Basti's that night.

Because Mitzi, the hottest chick I have ever met in my entire twenty-three years on this Earth, has balls. Figuratively, of course. Did I use that right? "Figuratively?"

Mitzi, beautiful Mitzi, has more balls tucked inside her lacy panties than any of us that night.

———

And just how beautiful Mitzi is, you ask?

Well, please allow me to at least make an attempt to describe her beauty, although I am sure that my words will surely fail.

I'll start with her name.

Mitzi is Marie Celine Gallofin Ricafort. Yes, she has two first names and two surnames like some fucking royalty. Princess Marie Celine Gallofin Ricafort, that's Mitzi for all of us, mere commoners within her court.

And here's the thing. That name actually matches her face and her, ummm, body.

The very first thing you'll notice about Mitzi is her lips.

God, those lips. If they say that eyes are the windows to the soul, Mitzi's lips are doors to...well...her. Restless is what I would describe them. Always a second away from either smiling or sneering. And this, not knowing whether she will smile or sneer, keeps you glued to her and wanting more.

Then there's her eyes. Big, bright eyes that see the world through a lens of wonder. And, if you look really closely, you could see sometimes, just sometimes, pain.

Her nose is engaged in a constant tug of war against her cheekbones as to which has the right to claim prominence on her face. Her pretty, perfect face. Ears, undefiled by any piercings are what I could describe as utilitarian. For tucking back her long wavy black hair always in need of a band or a clip or a tie but Mitzi just couldn't be bothered.

So that's Mitzi for you. No words can do her beauty some justice. Because she has the face and the height and the poise. Every time Mitzi enters into a room, the laws of physics get fucked up. Time slows down and gravity falters and sound is silenced.

Legend has it that in her sophomore year in her all-girls Catholic school, she happened to smile at a visiting priest and the reverend gave up the cloth, married some prostitute, and became a Satanist.

See? Mitzi deserves the name Marie Celine Gallofin Ricafort. And nothing could be truer: your name becomes you and you become the name. I shit you not.

Let me say it again: your name becomes you and you become the name.

But let's not get ahead of our story.

Basti leads Mitzi inside.

And as I have expected, molecules rearrange themselves around her presence and the chemistry of the entire penthouse undergoes a reaction.

It's true. Her entrance brightens up Basti's already blinding, white as fuck dig, dialing up its whiteness and sending it out of the color spectrum ever known to man. Photoshop would have to recalibrate its palette and Pantone would have to come up with a new color.

As I look at her, Basti gives Mitzi his welcome. A quick kiss on the mouth. Lips locking for the briefest of seconds. There are no tongues involved. At least, not that I can see.

That's how they are, don't ask. Because I can't even.

"Where's Pia?" Mitzi says.

"On the way with Vicente," Basti replies.

I get up from the sofa and give Mitzi an air kiss an inch away from her left cheek.

I smell her one-of-a-kind Mitzi smell and I have to confess, I get a mini hard on right there and then. What did I tell you about the laws of physics being useless in her midst? You know the feeling, right? The force did not really awaken but stirred for just a bit.

"Hey, Mitzi," I say. "I sent you a follower request on Insta?"

"When?" Mitzi says.

"Like, maybe three years ago," I say.

"Really? You're not licking my balls?" Mitzi says.

"Really." I say. "But no worries. You may accept it now."

"Insta is already canceled, Rafa," Mitzi says. "But don't worry, my lurve, I can send you a few nudes if you want. For some happy fapping. As long as you do me a liquid tribute."

Canceled? Ha. But I leave it at that.

———

As we all sit down on the sofa, Mitzi notices the weirdness right away.

"Basti," Mitzi says. "You are not recruiting us for some life insurance crap, right? Because for that, you need an Acer laptop and the venue of choice should be inside a KFC where you will treat us to a bucket of chicken."

Ohmyfuckinggods. That is precisely what's inside my mind this very second.

"Chill, people," Basti says. "It's a Friday."

"We should be drinking then!" This sentence is uttered by both Mitzi and me, in perfect synchronicity.

"What I have in mind is better than drinking," Basti says. He pauses and then adds, "And it is even better than the other thing that is not drinking."

Allow me to translate that: better than doing drugs. Or getting laid. Or maybe even both.

I have nothing to say to this, so I just stare into nothing and listen to the silence.

Chapter Ten

Rafa is silent like the ghost that he is.

Seeing him seated in the middle of @Basti's living room this Friday night had me interested. Intrigued. And to be honest, my lurves, inspired.

I know. I know. You haven't seen Rafa on all of my socials, much more IRL, and I need to do a proper intro. Because, manners.

So, here goes.

Rafa is Rafael Gutierrez.

And just how does this Rafa look?

Here's the first impression that you get from Rafa: he is average. Unremarkable also comes to mind. And another term is ordinary.

Now, this impression could be the effect of his face, because, like his clothes, it is unremarkable. And no, I am not being polite here. I am not trying to sugarcoat anything. I have been known in the biz to be brutally honest AF and I can say fugly to someone's face when he or she is indeed that fugly even if this said fugly is cast, crew, or even a client. Fugly is fugly and there is no denying that fact.

When I say unremarkable, what I mean is that Rafa's persona is Lower Middle Class. Or Socio-Economic Class C. Totes petit bourgeois *but on the right trajectory onto becoming a* nouveau riche.

Allow me to explain, my lurves.

His face is, to borrow a treatment from a film director that I've read in one of my pre-prods, cubist. Really, it's all right angles and sharp corners like a box that holds everything together and make them work.

Take his eyes. What seems uninterested on the surface will be revealed as actually inquisitive, those big brown eyes that do not project anything but record everything. But once you acknowledge that his eyes are framed by his face, they become average.

Or his cheeks. There's some promise there but, taken with his face, it remains a promise. Same with his nose, which could have been commanding, or his mouth, which could have been delicious IMHO, and his chin which could have projected strength. But his cubist face summarizes all these features and boxes them in and transforms them into something unremarkable.

And, just like any cubist work of art, what you see is not Rafa, per se, but the persona. Or, referencing back to cubism, what sticks in your mind is the movement and not the particular canvas that you are currently staring at, and in the case of Rafa's face, the movement of a petit bourgeois *towards a* nouveau riche *as I have already said.*

Take a look at Rafa and he is kinda cute.

Stare at him a second more and he is fuckable AF.

Stare at him too long and he is plain vanilla.

Now, let's go to his threads, in which I take a professional interest.

He is wearing a shirt and jeans ensemble with a cotton blazer that is not an atrocity for a Friday after hours. Really. The blazer is black, two-button, pressed, and spotless, not a single thread sticks out so far as I can see. His crew neck shirt is also black, no print, no creases, it looks brand new. His denims are selvage and get this, my lurves, he even got the three-inch fold right. Points where points are due. And for his kicks, he is wearing a Nike Presto React, in an all-black colorway from the sole to the laces, which, given that this is Rafa I am talking about, almost makes it dope.

That's Rafa for you. Almost adorbs, almost awesome. Almost.

His threads fit him and there seems to be no effort involved.

And if you take another look at Rafa you will see that he looks almost comfortable AF.

That is, until he sees me.

I know. I know.

It's not him, it's me.

I'm just a girl walking in front of a boy, wishing he will not ask me why I ghosted him years ago.

And so now, I come to answer the question.

Why the fuck have I ghosted Rafa?

But before you judge me, my lurves, please know that I only ghost hopeless people.

And Rafa is hopeless because he doesn't take his socials seriously. What I mean is that like any half-baked—fuck this word—influencer, he treats his social media presence like a side hustle.

K, not even like a side hustle. More of a hobby. He is but a mere dilettante, dipping his toes into the warm inviting waters of social media but never actually diving in. The worst. The way he treats Insta or Twitter or TikTok with the casual indif-

ference of a lurker actually borders on being criminal. He is basically murdering these platforms.

And no, this is not a dish out on the users who do normcore. I dig normcore. I really do. Normcore is a movement unto itself and is one of the most interesting shit out there.

What Rafa does is real life.

And nothing kills social media more than real life.

See? Rafa is hopeless. Beyond salvation. Dead as fucking dead.

I was the first to ghost him but soon enough, we, to mean @Basti, @Pia, and @Vicente all go dark on Rafa.

@Basti can really liven up a Friday night, even a stormy Friday night such as this, but I have not a clue that tonight, it will involve Rafa.

I haven't expected this. The way I haven't expected any other shit that @Basti has unleashed on previous Fridays. There was this one time when we had midget wrestlers doing a no-holds-barred fight-to-the-death mixed martial arts spectacle right in this very living room. You've seen my snaps, right? And who can forget our fashion show, runway and all, as he did that Lady Gaga retrospective. Shame on you if you haven't seen it. It was one of my best livestreams ever and I still have the digits and the dollars to prove it. Even landed me a couple of gigs. And elite talent agencies in the US, the three-lettered ones, dropped me a DM, offering representation. I said no of course because I am not an—fuck this word—influencer.

But let's go back to Rafa, my lurves.

So he is seated on the white sofa and the first thing he does after he greets me on one—one!—cheek with a kiss, is to ask why I have ignored his request on Insta. Like, since forevs.

I give him my usual non-answer.

I tell him Insta is canceled.

And then I tease him with a few nudes.
This shuts him up.
I settle on the sofa.
And this is when I notice that there is something very
weird with the fucking silence.

Chapter Eleven

Have you ever done that? Listen to the silence? It's not a very pleasant experience, believe you me.

Silence will mess with your head. With the lack of music that usually layers any activity in Basti's crib, I could hear the faint humming of the wine fridge. The rhythmic murmur of the AC. I could hear, no feel, the electricity crawling through the wires and charging the air.

I could even feel the storm that has been hovering the entire afternoon gather its strength and prepare to strike.

I could also feel something.

Some *other* thing that my mind just cannot process into words this time.

I could feel...a presence.

Mitzi's voice interrupts my thoughts.

"Basti," I hear her say. "If nothing is happening here, I

have to get going before the storm comes. You've got a very cool place and all, plus you know that I lurve you to death, but I can't waste my Friday night doing this. Whatever this is."

Mitzi gets up from the sofa and snaps a couple of selfies with her iPhone.

And then she turns to me.

"Rafa?" Mitzi says.

I immediately stand up because hearing my name spoken by Mitzi is one of the greatest things ever.

Allow me to explain.

Mitzi and I have some kind of, ummm, history.

She used to be my BAE. And I used to be her lurve. We used to be together. We've done things together. And most of the things that we've done together started with that question, "Rafa?"

Spoken by Mitzi, my name plus a question mark is both a command and a promise.

As in: "Rafael, come with me this very second and I will do some shit to you that you would never have thought I could do. And I would do it at least once. And that means that there might be a chance I would do it a second time. Maybe more."

Ohmyfuckinggods.

If only I could tell you what "Rafa?" has led to. But, as my Lolo used to say, a gentleman never tells. And what am I if not a gentleman?

We've done a lot of shit, Mitzi and me. She is the very reason I currently do not have an honest relationship with a girl and maybe will never have, ever again.

The doorbell dings.

Basti heads to the door and Pia enters followed by Vicente.

Basti being Basti, welcomes his girlfriend of two? three? years the same way he greets Vicente.

No, not with a kiss on the lips, you fucking perverts! With a fist bump!

Pia immediately sashays toward Mitzi while Basti and Vicente talk about vinyl. The first pressing of The Dark Side of the Moon or some crap like that. This, despite the AKAI being silent as the fucking dead.

At the sofa, Pia starts the pleasantries with Mitzi.

"Who's the latest celebrity that you've styled?" Pia says.

Mitzi, as I have said, does some fashion styling but don't you ever call her a fashion stylist. Sometimes, just sometimes, she also wears the clothes she is purveying but you're not allowed to call her a model, a brand ambassador, or heaven forbid, a content creator. She really hates these fucking words. She also does a ton of shit on the internet, mostly on social media, but it is forbidden to call her a web entrepreneur, a vlogger, or that icky, slimy, greasy word, that really drives her mental as fuck, influencer.

So, what is she, you may ask?

Well, please allow me to answer that.

Mitzi is a free spirit. Her words, not mine.

Anyway, the translation to Pia's greeting is: "How busy are you pretending to have a job?"

Remember, both Mitzi and Pia, like Basti and Vicente, are in their own family business. Currently. And always have been. And always will be.

Mitzi names a couple of *telenobela* stars doing a TV ad campaign and one Hollywood has-been currently in town to promote a casino. And then she launches her very own offensive.

"I'm glad you and Vicente came. I was just about to leave. How's the traffic? Is it raining yet?"

This early in the evening, that girl talk has yet to be translated into human language. But, patience, my friends, things will become very clear as to what Mitzi has uttered as we continue our story.

Pia whips out her iPhone.

Poses.

Snaps a selfie.

After a couple of safety shots, she and Mitzi take turns in taking the photos.

This is followed by the two of them squeezing into the frame for more shots.

This is followed by short vids of them kissing the cam. Then each other. First, on the cheeks, and finally, on the lips.

Yes, with tongues. Lots of tongues. And a trail or two of saliva.

Ladies and gentlemen, gays and lesbos, and those of you who are either curious or confiiirrrmmmed, it is at this precise moment that I get a full erection.

The fucking force has been awakened.

In my pants, I feel...a presence.

Both of these beauties delete shots, edit the survivors, and update their social media. I'm guessing Facebook and Twitter and Instagram and TikTok and Snapchat. The short vids I'm guessing as chaste teasers on YouTube directing their paying public to PornHub and OnlyFans.

Yep, there's no such thing as a free pussy shot to these two beauties.

Well, except for Basti and Vicente and me because what's a few nudes between friends, amirite?

To continue.

After a lifetime of staring, they finally notice me.

Mitzi heads to my right side and Pia pirouettes to my left.

Each of them takes a token shot.

The same token shot with Mitzi and Pia kissing me on either cheek, my face in a grimace, doing my best to pretend that I am suffering from these two barbies assaulting me with affection, fake or maybe not, I really couldn't be sure. But deep inside, I am honestly hoping that this was real.

Or "for realz," as Pia would say.

I whipped out my iPhone so that I could also take a shot, just a single shot, but the Mitzi and Pia are done. I pocket my phone without snapping a single photo.

The three of us sit down.

I give Pia the same air kiss that I gave Mitzi.

I smell sex on her, that unique woman smell that comes with the afterglow, offensive and intoxicating at the same time. My erection is about to go nuclear. I get a little moist with pre-cum.

Think. And think fast, I tell myself.

"About that Insta..." I say.

"Insta?" Pia says.

"I've sent you a request," I say. "About two, maybe three years ago."

"What?!" Pia says. And get this, she sounds genuinely surprised. "Ohhheeemgeee! For realz?! You're not sucking my dick?!"

"Really," I say.

"Ha! #InstaRIP has trended like, four years ago, Rafa!" Pia says. "But baby, I just got a vagacial if you want a few shots for your spank bank. Close ups. Or if you want, medium shots with my face in the frame."

I leave it at that.

"Anyway, how's life?" Pia says. This after, hearting a couple of shots on her Insta.

And the translation of the comment is: "You're still alive, Rafa. You still exist. You are on my radar. Let's see how things go after I get tired of Basti."

See, Pia and I don't have a history.

Yet, I always tell myself. She was the one who got away. Or is getting away, I always tell myself that, too.

Because "Rafa?" is to Mitzi as "How's life?" is to Pia. It

gives me so much hope, that question, because there is a chance, no matter how small, that I might still avoid the gaping, sharp-toothed jaws of The Friend Zone.

Mitzi and Pia are my two precious BAEs.

The one and only true loves of my life.

My 'til death do us parts.

Pia is Pia de la Fuente.

I am not sure if it is Clitopia or Procopia and I never dared to ask. Someday if she marries me, I might finally get to see her birth certificate and as of now, I am willing to make her given name a mystery. But if you ask me, I would really prefer Clitopia. For having a girlfriend whose name is a mix of the words "clitoris" and "utopia" can work on so many levels.

And how does this Pia de la Fuente look?

Again, please allow me to make an attempt in painting her angelic being using words.

She is also beautiful as fuck. In a studied kind of way. Like she is making a career of looking stunning and is succeeding in doing it, even exceeding expectations. Pia is well put together. Perfection well deserved.

The first thing you notice about Pia is her forehead. No, it's not wide or spacious or anything like that. It is as the word is, a forehead. Like the thing that comes before the rest of her head and her body and her person.

And with this forehead, Pia is indeed introduced. Her long and luscious hair that is always tied in a Samurai bun, you know, that hairstyle popularized by hipsters in Brooklyn about a dozen years ago. Pia's knot is neither too tight nor too loose, always with a few strands dangling across her face.

There's Pia's eyes. If you've ever seen a cat's pair of eyes, you've seen Pia's. Feline eyes, that's what Pia has. No, she doesn't have slits for pupils but the same zero fucks given look is there. Her eyes do not invite you into her soul. They languidly ignore your attempt.

As for her lips, I am going to resort to a cliché. Kissable lips. This description has been done to death, I know, but her lips are not just plump but always a bit opened as if she is about to kiss someone. And from these perpetually opened lips, you may be treated with a sight of her tongue slowly slithering out of her mouth to moisten them. That is, if luck is on your side.

The rest of her features are locked in constant competition with these lips. Her small but tall nose, her nondescript ears always adorned with bejeweled earrings, her soft chin, and her cheeks with a hint of dimples when she smiles. Her thin neck that adds inches to her height and subtracts a few kilos off her weight on her already painfully thin frame.

If Mitzi wears dude clothes over her lace thongs that she let me keep as souvenirs way back when, Pia wears grown-up clothes. No, let me correct that. Pia does not wear clothes, instead, she models them.

Grown-up clothes. But not the blouses and the *bestidas* the *Titas* of Manila who have given up on life wear with pride. Or the young MILFs with their weaponized strollers forever strutting their sagging asses in see-through Lululemons. What Pia models are real clothes for a real woman.

This Friday, Pia is wearing a matte gray dress, something asymmetrical that starts loose on top and tightens down as it wraps her feet with a neckline that opens and favors the right shoulder exposing a very thin purple bra strap. So stylish.

And then there are the shoes. The French red-soled ones that I can never quite properly pronounce.

See? Pia is a beauty.

If Mitzi's presence alters the physical and chemical properties of a place, Pia triggers a chain reaction from people. She is a walking and talking and breathing stimulus that commands a response.

Whenever Pia graces a room with her being, mouths are opened, dumbs are struck, flabbers are gasted.

And, as is always the case with me, dicks are hardened.

She also has her own urban legend. It is whispered in the international beauty competition circuit that Pia once competed in the Miss Philippines beauty contest and every single contestant who joined that year became lesbians and a couple even lost their sanities with one making an unsuccessful attempt at suicide.

I already told you right? My force is awakened. That's Pia for you.

———

Now, let's circle back to Pia's question.

"Life," I say. And not minding whether she gets the reference, I add, "Same shit. Different day."

This is just a throwaway line I direct at her. I know that she doesn't hear it. Doesn't care to hear it. There are more important things in Pia's life for her to be bothered by trivialities like what I have to say.

Important things like equality. That's why she is a very active participant in her family business like the rest of her brothers. She deserves, no, I think the word that Pia used was "entitled" to her share of her family's wealth.

Important things like health. That's why she is always on these latest diets. Pia is the only vegan I know who is also allergic to gluten and is lactose intolerant. She also avoids anything genetically modified. Pia's meals are mostly what Mitzi calls "The French Breakfast," herself being a proponent and practitioner of it as well. See those posters on Basti's wall by the Bruce Lee toys? Pia could light a cigarette—and I mean a Marl red and not that vape shit that looks stupid as fuck—as she stares at the artwork and then calls it breakfast. Lunch and dinner too if she is having a busy day. And yes, being in the family business means being busy on a regular basis. She once boasted that she invented intermittent fasting and I totally believe her.

Important things like living in the moment. That's why her phone is always snapping away all these photos so she can update her feeds 24/7/365 like a reality show unfolding in real-time.

Important things like commitment. That's why she is fucking as many dudes as she can now, because, and again these are her words, "I want to be absolutely committed to the man whom I will love when I finally decide to settle down and start a family."

Who can help themselves not to fall in love with Pia? Certainly not Basti.

Certainly not me.

And so, I just surrender to the silence.

Chapter Twelve

S ilence.
    This silence.
    This fucking silence!
At first, I try to push it out of my head.
Only to discover that I couldn't.
Because this silence is not within the confines of my mind but is in the room with us this Friday night.
This silence is awake.
This silence is somehow alive.
I try to get a feel for it, to find it, to name it.
I listen to the silence.
And here's the thing, my lurves.
I feel that this silence is listening to me.

Now, my lurves, I dare you to try it.
    Listen.
    Just listen to the silence.
    You don't have to do anything, just listen for that silence that surrounds you.

That silence that is on your left, on your right, in front of you.

That silence that is behind you.

That silence that is smothering you from above.

That silence that is creeping up from way down below, its tentacles ever so slowly encircling your thighs as it inches upwards to your waiting wet cunt.

That silence that has always been with you.

That silence that will be with you long after I'm done with my story and you have come to the end.

Just listen.

There is a silence.

And this silence will not be silenced.

I call out @Basti's name just to fill the room with something. Anything but this fucking silence like an inverse soundtrack of something sinister, a backmasked music bed of menace permeating the entire penthouse.

I tell him that my awesomeness doesn't do Fridays like this and that I have somewhere else to go.

While waiting for his reply, I snap a couple of selfies to distract myself. Because, moments. Also, Insta. And, this story.

"Rafa?" I say aloud when @Basti does not answer.

I'm fairly sure that Rafa is being weirded out by the silence too and is dying to get the fuck out of this place.

Rafa immediately stands up as he hears his name being spoken by moi.

Now, I have to fess up, my lurves.

I am sure that by merely calling his name, Rafa will help me flee this silence because, well, I used to fuck him.

Like, we used to be a thing.

As in, for a short while, he was my one true lurve.

I know. I know.

This might be the real reason that I ghosted Rafa, but whatevs.

All I know is that he still is not over me and maybe never will be, as, from his look earlier, he seems to have been nursing his little heartbreak ever since we've broken up IRL. If I hadn't known him before, I could have sworn that what I got was a look from someone who knows he can never have me, ever.

It's so fucking sad.

It's so totes adorbs.

Here's another free piece of advice, my lurves: find yourself a BAE who looks at you the way Rafa looks at me and you're all set for a lifetime of orgasms and awesomeness.

And I can't even say that Rafa is giving me this kind of look because of my beauty. No, I will never say that. I can also do modesty, remember?

It's just that Rafa is one of those dudes whom I have had the pleasure of devirginizing, so I guess it might have meant something to him.

Or, because I'm really modest, I might have meant something to him. That there might be some meaning beyond my making him cum once upon a happier time.

And get this, my lurves, when I deflowered Rafa, the pleasure was all mine. Just between us, my lurves, what happened was that we totally skipped the wining and dining and went straight to the sixty-nining, how awesome is that?

And so, what I did right after that unforgettable fuck was to fuck him again. And again. And again.

I fucked him so much and so hard and so often that we even developed our very own inside joke.

Whenever I took his erection in my hand, I would always ask: "Whose gigantic dick is this? This could not be yours!"

And Rafa would always reply: "This dick is mine, but I seriously think it is possessed!"

This joke never failed to give us both a laugh.

And after the fucking with all the joking? Well, all I had to do was this one thing. Call him by his name. But the trick is to make it more like a question than a command.

Here's another secret of the biz, my lurves: rather than tell your audience what to do, engage them. Everyone responds to a question more than they do with a command. That's why all those question stickers were invented on Insta. And the surveys on Twitter.

Anyhoo.

"Rafa?"

See? A question and not a command. Spoken by moi, this has resulted in many other things—of which a few of them are wholesome, sort of, and most may even be legal, sort of—that we've done once, only to do it again for a second, and a third, well, you get the idea, my lurves.

Just thinking about it now is making me moist AF.

Thankfully, the doorbell dings.

It is @Pia.

You all know @Pia from my socials, right?

We're like BFFs, @Pia and me and that's why you always see her on my feeds, the way I am always on hers. She even guests on my OnlyFans every now and then, and I must say, she is almost as good as me in bed. A lot of my loyal fans actually DM me to ask if we are lovers IRL. My standard reply is a tease, of course, just enough hint that we might be involved.

Again, here's another secret in the biz: the infinite scroll. That would be making the tease never ending so that the users always come back for more. It's like edging, my lurves, which, according to anals and algos, is my best rated category ever, both on PornHub and on OnlyFans. It is the promise of a climax that makes it worthwhile. My orgasm could be real, or it could even be ruined, or it could be fake or it could even be fab, but my loyal fans pay for my journey to get there. Forever teasing you, that's moi.

Take this story, my lurves. You keep reading because I am forever teasing you with a climax. I am edging you with words, keeping you hard and moist. That I just make the scenes up as I go along or will totally drop an ending from way left field does not matter. It is the getting there that is the fucking there.

Anyhoo.

The answer to the question as to why @Pia and me could never be lovers IRL. The truth is that aside from the fact that I am not a vagitarian except on some of my OnlyFans vids, @Basti and @Pia are a thing. Girl code, I know. They've been BAEs for about three years now. They are totes in lurve and the cutest couple ever. The silly little heartbreaker and the adorable little slut.

This Friday night, @Pia is even dressed for the part.

And I say this, my lurves, because she is wearing a dress. To use her very own words, "for realz." There is something really off with the off-shoulder cut that she is wearing, like that old joke between tailors, that one about asking the other whether he has run out of fabric while making a dress and he replied that it's creativity that he has run out of. But @Pia carries it well, as per yoozh, despite the major WIP vibe. I know that this particular dress is yet to hit the racks as this was one of the Friday projects I said no to about six months ago. Which gets me to ask myself whether Pia is being paid to wear it as an—fuck this word—influencer. Or, gods forbid, whether she got it from a swag. L'horreur! Hasn't she heard the general fucking principle? You are not supposed to get high on your own supply. But she's the one wearing that atrocity of an OOTD, so whatevs.

@Pia always decorates her ears with something shiny the way a magician deploys a finely calibrated misdirection so that your eyes are drawn to where they should be going. In her case, away from her forehead and onto her thin neck. And her ever-present earrings are the props to this magic show. She blings it

like it has never been blung before. This Friday night, she is wearing a pair of diamond-encrusted earrings, Soleste by Tiffany. With rocks bigger than her barely concealed pimples. Now, she will never wear a knock-off, so, my best guess is that she just had a spat with her Mommy and @Pia pilfered the pair out of spite.

On her feet is a pair of Louboutin's. Which is perfectly on brand, it being the official footwear of high-end Hollywood hoes. And not only that. Seeing the pair on her feet makes the brand even more unchristian. The five-inch heels elevate @Pia from the adorable little slut to the great tribulation harlot. @Pia is the ho in holy. A shoutout to Sister Heidi, a religious nun compared to @Pia who is a religious none. Yep, Sister Heidi was the one who introduced me to l'horreur that is the Book of Revelations, her favorite book of le Bible.

@Pia heads over and my sense of smell gets majorly messed up by her fragrance. It is something I just cannot place. Like Another 13, that eau de parfum by Le Labo, but layered with another scent, I honestly cannot say what, my lurves. Maybe 'ija de puta, although while very feminine, is not very French. Whatevs. All I can say is that there is a very subtle hint of deceit in that well-rounded bouquet of desperation.

Anyhoo.

@Pia heads over and as per yoozh, she asks me about my current projects.

I tell her my latest gig, the has-been at the casino, because aside from modesty, I can also do the humblebrag.

But I know that she doesn't really care about this thing, this having a real paying job in Benjamins, no less, because @Pia is the real deal. And by that, I mean that her fakery of being a fully fledged—fuck this word—influencer is real as fuck.

Or that would be, in @Pia's very own words, "for realz."

It's either influencing or nothing.

It's either Insta or nada.

It's either friend me or fuck you.

Take what she is doing this very Friday night.

I sling her a question about whether it is raining yet and as per yoozh, she does not get the hint. Or pretends not to get the hint. Instead, she whips out her iPhone, does the pose that shows her best angle—chin a bit up and her face tilted to the left to hide her ginormous forehead—and starts to take some selfies.

She invites me to join her and together we take turns in taking the shots, posing this way and that, giving the camera an overload in so much awesomeness it is a mystery as to why that iPhone does not lose its mind and break, its sleek surface shattering and its hi-tech innards smoldering.

The frame can't contain our beautiful faces that we have to squeeze in and squeeze in some more.

@Pia kisses me, sweet, chaste kisses, the kind that Sister Heidi would just frown upon instead of hauling my ass to the principal during my Catholic schooling.

I kiss @Pia back.

With tongue this time.

Exactly how I did it with @Basti earlier.

As we continue Frenching each other, I take out my iPhone. For a couple of my own shots. And vids of course. Plus, the very important safety shots.

Again, here is another secret of the biz. Take a note of this secret, my lurves, screenshot these very words and save it in the iCloud of your brain for this is the one secret in the biz that is worth learning. And I will be going back to this one secret before my story is done.

Here, my lurves, is the secret: take a safety shot. Always.

I heard a film director say once that it is the B-rolls that have saved many a film or photography project. That what is happening behind the scenes is what carries the story, but only when it is captured and reworked back into the narrative during the edit.

Or in the words of a cinematographer, the information area is just as important as the frame. Every time you frame a shot, *think beyond that frame. Literally, think outside of that box. Or as @Pia would say, "for realz." Give yourself some leeway. Because you can't edit back into the picture what is outside of the frame.*

Ever wonder why all of my Insta posts are perfect as fuck, my lurves?

Yep, safety shots.

Again: take a safety shot. Always.

Anyhoo.

After we somehow manage to untangle our tongues, @Pia and I take a break to catch our breath and check our socials. I delete a few shots and save my drafts and she does hers. And because we are pros AF, we both ignore our feeds. It is already after hours on a Friday and who gives a shit about an amateur snap of a noob's cocktail drink? Or a follower request from someone named Jubylyn of Tagbilaran? Or a devious mention from a brand manager of a vaginal wash asking me if I want to be a brand ambassador?

I put my iPhone to sleep and this is when I once again notice Rafa.

He is still on the sofa looking at me like a rescue puppy afflicted with a bad case of sepanx needing adoption from one of those PETA ads during Christmas. So sad. So adorbs. And because it is Rafa, after a second of his stare, it just becomes so unbearable.

Thankfully, his gaze shifts from me to @Pia.

You should have seen his face, my lurves.

Now, as I continue with my story, think of what I am about to tell you as a DM. It is just between you and moi. Nobody knows this and nobody needs to know. Really. This is a super duper secret.

K? Swear to gods and hope to die?

K.

Here's the thing, my lurves: I am getting the major vibe that Rafa, while still very much in lurve with me, also has the hots for @Pia.

There.

My little lost puppy is in lurve with someone else who just happens to be that adorable little slut, @Pia. Who, let us not forget, is very much involved with @Basti.

I know. I know.

It's a bit sus of moi, feeling this, telling you this, when Rafa and me used to be a thing. And that I was the one who dumped him.

And ghosted him.

Then again, Rafa must at the very fucking least, respect the Bro Code. The fucking Bro Code.

Now, seeing Rafa's face salivating from both @Pia's and my awesomeness is breaking my heart into a million little pieces.

I decide to do a mini pity party and invite Rafa for a couple of groufies. @Pia and me sandwich Rafa and pretend to kiss him on either cheek as we both do the snaps using our own iPhones.

@Pia and me do a round of safety shots but stop as soon as Rafa brings out his iPhone. We are pros, remember?

And not only that, this Friday night, Rafa is still a ghost. We both wouldn't wanna be caught dead with our faces on any of his snaps. Because what if he uploads them on his Insta? Or Twitter? Or FB? And tags us? See? We might as well be dead.

The three of us sit down on the white sofa, all our iPhones asleep and forgotten.

Rafa, as I have expected, asks @Pia about his follower request on her Insta. And as I have also expected, she shoots him down. That Insta has already been canceled awhile back. Of course, she also does my shtick of offering him a few nudes, mentioning something about a vagacial. Such a tease, this adorable little slut.

Nonetheless, I also wonder: is @Pia also getting moist from the way Rafa looks at her?

I know. I know.

This is so not me to get insecure and shit but fuck, I know @Pia.

Especially when, on this Friday night of all Friday nights of not seeing him, she asks Rafa this very question: "How's life?"

"How's life?"

Such an innocent question, right?

It's up there with asking someone about the weather.

But here's the scoop, my lurves.

There is not a single thing that is innocent about @Pia.

"How's life?"

It's a question everyone asks without really giving a shit about the answer. And only if one does bother to provide an answer. Because, really, how would you even answer that?

"How's life?"

Coming from @Pia, this really means that she doesn't care about yours. Really. Or, in her very own words, that would be, "for realz."

Because why ever would she care about your pathetic little life when hers is just perfect AF.

"How's life?"

The unspoken words are: "My life is perfect why should I give a shit about yours?"

Just look at @Pia's socials, my lurves.

All of her posts in all of her feeds are all about flaunting her moolah while at the same time flogging vaginal wash to the middle class. The message is, to quote one of the photographers I've worked with on an ad campaign, is the medium. Or, if I may bastardize that, the messenger is the medium. And @Pia's message is: look at this awesome life you can never have, these gourmet foods you will never taste, these vacations you will never take and, while you're at it, check out this vaginal wash at a discounted price. But first you must heart me.

"How's life?"

To @Pia, everything is about her life.

"How's life?"

To @Pia, this only means one thing.

That she is, totes magotes, fucking Rafa before this Friday is done.

And just how do I know this?

Because "How's life?" is @Pia's line to my very own "Rafa?"

In the biz, we call this the call to action.

"How's life?"

This is how @Pia hooked @Basti.

And this is also how that adorable little slut is hooking up with Rafa.

And not only that, my lurves, I have this sus that this is how she is also totally hooking up with @Vicente.

Chapter Thirteen

Ah, Vicente. Vicente is Vicente Pascual.

Okay. I think words are really going to fail me this time. "Literally," as Pia would say. But I have to give it a go if we have to continue with our story.

So here goes.

The very first thing you notice about Vicente is that he is the only one in our small group of young degenerates and beautiful reprobates who wears what Mitzi has termed as "Couture: Unemployed." This, Vicente's look, is something that she actually used as an inspiration in one of her fashion styling projects.

And this is the look: Vicente basically just wears whatever it is that he can get his hands on.

This Friday night, he is in crumpled long sleeves that's either a very dull gray or a very dirty white, pink shorts, and beat-up Birks. Basically, he looks like he doesn't give a shit, which, really is the case.

But here's the fucking thing. Vicente can pull it off. "Literally," as Pia would attest.

Why? Because he is another good-looking motherfucker, even with his hair being currently chased by a dozen scissor-wielding barbers. Or, that would be creative directors if high-end hair salons are your thing.

Much like his unkempt clothes, his unkempt hair also works magically with his face and his physique.

Vicente has a face that one could only describe as "punch-able." Basti would rather use the word "Atenean," you know, from that Catholic school of coño fuckers and fuckerettes but really, the correct terminology is "punchable." As in, if he is not your friend, you would want to punch Vicente's face. And punch it real hard.

I really can't explain it but maybe it's the eager-to-please face. His eyes forever set too bright and always looking at yours like some fucking portrait of Jesus Christ in your Lola's bedroom. His lips that easily give to smiling and laughing and agreeing make you wonder whether he is sincere or sarcastic. Fluffy cheeks that are very Schreiberesque like that Holly-wood actor or very Putinesque like that fucker in Russia. A tall nose and a strong chin balance these cheeks and solidify his face into a very gorgeous dude.

And that's not mentioning that he has one of those bodies that, at least for now, doesn't need to go to the gym to be main-tained. You might know the type. No abs but no flabs either. Like one of those seventies stoner rockers on the back covers of Basti's vinyls.

The second thing you notice about Vicente is the way he speaks.

"Vicente," I say when he and Basti head over to the sofa as soon they're done talking shit about records. "You need to accept my Insta request, dude. It's been suffering in limbo for about a year or two."

"Wha—?! Listen very carefully, my friend. Vicente says you weren't invited to the #InstaIsOverParty."

I leave it at that.

At least he did not offer me a fucking dick pic.

And yes, Vicente is one of the very few people on this planet who still refers to himself in the fucking third person. Like a comic book villain.

I can't honestly say if what he is doing is just an affectation, a phase, something he will grow out of, but if you ask me, I think Vicente is just a fucking retard. Seriously.

It sounds a bit weird at first, but you get used to it. At least we are so used to it that we no longer give it a thought. Like a foreign accent that you get accustomed to. Or a speech defect that no longer irritates.

For the record, I have my list of Vicente's greatest unforgettable hits: "Vicente does not approve." And "Vicente thinks that we should cease this faggotry at once." And "Vicente says fuck you."

Vicente referring to himself in the third person is very important in our story.

Because, yes, if there is one person in the room who will signify that shit is already starting this Friday, that would be Vicente.

Chapter Fourteen

@ Vicente.
You've all seen him in my socials, right, my lurves?

I am not going to sabotage my story by boring you to death with how he looks or how he dresses. Engagement, after all, is key. Both in Insta and in this story. My story.

Sure, he is also hot in his own weird way but he dresses like a fucking slob who just couldn't be bothered. So, I am not even going to make an attempt in describing the fucking obscenity of what he is wearing this Friday. Let me just say that if @Basti has a dress code that says corner office, @Vicente has one, too. And it says the coroner's office.

All you need to know about @Vicente, my lurves, is how he speaks.

"Vicente does not approve."

And...

"Vicente thinks we should cease this faggotry at once."

And...

"Vicente says fuck you."

Correct, my lurves.

@Vicente speaks in the third.

Like he is having an out of body experience.

You know me, my lurves. I don't do collabs. I also don't do cross-posts. I don't do fucking shoutouts. Well, except for Sister Heidi because she deserves credit for teaching us l'horreur that is the Book of Revelations.

Anyhoo.

@Vicente and how he fucking speaks in the third is very important in my story.

Because this Friday night really starts with that lousy little retard @Vicente.

Yep, my lurves, I have to fess up. This particular Friday in my story does not begin with my awesome set of skills called self-marketing.

Chapter Fifteen

S elf-marketing.
These two words are the best words that explain the Insta shit that keeps happening.

I know you all have been wondering why everyone keeps blowing me off every time I remind them that they have yet to accept my follower requests. Requests that have been sent and continually ignored since, like, forever.

Okay. Here goes.

All of us are on social media. You know, like any other person who pretends he or she doesn't want to be cool, ever.

But...

But!

But here's the fucking thing.

Basti, Vicente, Pia, and Mitzi have real social media presence.

A presence.

They fucking exist on Insta, Facebook, Twitter, TikTok, YouTube, Snapchat and whatever platform of self-marketing is out there.

And, if you know how to forage the fucking internet of

turds, you may even find the one and only loves of my life on
PornHub. Most certainly on OnlyFans.

They have friends, followers, fans. In the fucking millions,
believe you me. Per account.

And all these fuckers and fuckerettes, these fawning fans,
have self-anointed names like any legit celebrity-worshipping
community.

Basti has his Bastirds.

Mostly, these are the bros salivating over his hipster lifestyle. Everything is either cool or lit or sick as fuck to them. A
few babes follow him, of course, but only those hoping to snag
for themselves a moneyed husband or, as a last resort, a baby
papa. Basti is what you would call an internet native. He was
on Reddit before Redditors became a thing. He wandered
through various obscure communities, lurked in finance
forums, hung around in r/fuckwallstreet where he fucked the
short sellers and beat them at their own game by making dumb
money cool and individual investors even cooler. As his
preferred stocks propelled prices to the stratosphere, so did his
upvotes. His followers earned untold fortunes while he got
anonymous fame. I'm sure he also raked in millions and more
but Basti would never discuss it because this is his shit: money
talks, wealth keeps quiet. To mean, the wealthy class does not
talk about wealth, all they do is manage their wealth. His next
move was to dox himself on Insta where he became a fucking
rockstar. The leet behind the Reddit username outed his own
identity. How lit is that? Even more puzzling was his next
move. He migrated his presence from Insta to, you will not
fucking believe this, LinkedIn, where, to this very Friday, he
lords over like a kingmaker dispensing insider information and
creating exclusive connections to the tech bro fuckers and the
hedge fund assholes and the stock market douchebags despite
being unfuckingemployed. It is rumored in the consulting
circuit that getting linked to Basti guarantees an instant promotion and a performance bonus. Now isn't that ironic? It's gotta

be ironic, right? His nickname in the corporate world, the very same world that he despises as much as he loathes his parents, stopped from being "The Scion" and morphed into "The Seer."

Vicente has his Victims.

These are the bruhs, the Reddit rejects, the techie trolls who respond to his posts in the same retardese that is the third person. Retarded little fuckers. He's also got some babes too, only because insanity is gender-neutral and an equal-opportunity sucker. Annoying little fuckerettes, all of them are. Yes, Vicente also started his presence on Insta, developed his fanbase there, migrated to Reddit where his lunacy attracted even more eyeballs, then when this retard got kicked out for posting all kinds of insensitive content, he packed up and moved on to 8Chan, and got kicked out, too. I know, what shit do you have to do to get kicked out of 8Chan? Really, I am curious! And so, he migrated over and monetized his followers to YouTube and Twitch where he livestreams his retarded thoughts on games and consoles, music and gears, vintage and emerging tech. His format is the "let's take this shit apart and see what lies inside" schtick, like Mythbusters for noobs but his performance art is what delivers the traffic. He swears in the third person like a motherfucker all throughout the show and can only get away with it because there is a Parental Guidance: Explicit Language disclaimer in every episode and he has already established that he is not right in the head. His channel is *Vicente is One Angry Fucker* Visit at your own peril. You have been warned.

Pia has The Pipol.

Ah, this needs to be unpacked. First, we have the dudettes, they are the pre-teens, teens, and twenty-somethings whose online activism is buying whatever it is that Pia is shilling at the moment. For these fans, the struggle is real when it comes to buying the latest object of desire that Pia posts. And believe you me, Pia can sell something out with a single tweet. This is where her presence began, Twitter. Pia is one of those who, from the early aughts of social media, read correctly that for her to really influence, she need not follow anyone. Be they celebrities. Or brands. She is the celebrity. She is the brand. She also never retweets, quotes, or likes any other account. From Twitter to Insta to TikTok, she has zero following but millions of followers. Haute influencing at its purest. She knows that the more she is snobbish AF, the more her fans will want her. What she is doing is basically monetizing Stockholm Syndrome. And then there are The Pipol who are the dudes. These are her secondary market segment and yes, the dudes also rake in the moolah via Pia's PornHub and OnlyFans presence. Of course, she knows that they are fapping off to her, but she loves this knowledge, for what she sees are the tributes. And by that she means the cash and not the jizz that most of her fans sling back at her in dick pics as proof of subscription purchase. Mostly, these are teens but a few D.O.M.s are fans as well. A proposal surfaces now and then in the comments section and Pia, being a real web entrepreneur, is sweet enough to reply with a very gracious "no" to each and every single one of them but hints that there might be a "yes" somewhere on the horizon. See? Pia is the pro in prostitute.

Mitzi has Mitziztahs.

I know, this is a misnomer. Sexist even. Maybe homophobic? But the origin story of her fanbase explains this. Remember when Pia flirted with the Miss Philippines beauty contest? The very same one where it was rumored that all other contestants became lesbians and one even attempted suicide? Well, Mitzi made a comment on one of Pia's Twitter posts during the evening gown competition and this comment got picked up by the *Ates* of the *Federasyon*. This one innocent comment was retweeted a hundred million times and what is supposed to be an innocent, unscripted girl crush was hijacked by the gay community who created a rivalry between these two beauties inside the permeable wall of the Twitterverse where none exists IRL. Thus, the Mitziztahs were birthed. Mitzi, like Pia, was aware enough to realize that with a fanbase this solid, well, how easy would it be to part them from their money? A totally manufactured online spat started between the two BFFs, raking in serious offline dough that Mitzi never minded. Neither did she rebaptize the Mitziztahs. What she did was to corral her diehard fans and lock them onto Twitter where the Battle of the Beauties continues to this very minute. The rest, she siphoned and shepherded to her other social media accounts as she widened her platforms, diversified her online offerings, and broadened her target market. Mitzi, the stylist, vlogger, and influencer was born. On Insta, YouTube, and TikTok. She can sell anything and everything, but the one commodity that continues to be a best-seller is her persona of being a free spirit who sells her body at a premium price on OnlyFans. Her fans lap that shit up the way they fap to her vids. Who doesn't want to see a free spirit in the nude? And so, a porn star was born. And yes, just like Pia, Mitzi follows not a single person on all her socials. If that's not being a free spirit, I don't know what the fuck is.

There it is.

Compared to their presence and fanbase, I am nothing. I do not exist.

I am a fucking ghost.

This lack of presence on the internet is the reason why they keep blowing me off every time I remind them that they have yet to accept my follower request.

You've heard what they keep saying.

"#InstaIsCanceled."

"#InstaIsOverParty."

"#RIPInsta."

And that very dismissive "Social media is dead."

Yep. Dead as fucking dead.

Sometimes, though, they also take the time to explain why I can never be their fan.

"Men...you have to move on." This is from Basti. Of course, like most of his thoughts, he doesn't complete this one. Move on to where? I would have settled with "...real life awaits," but no, nothing follows.

"Vicente is never on Insta." From you know who. Even though everyone knows that he only posts semi-nude snaps of Pia with the barest hint of her very cute nipples or her freshly shaven pussy, all layered with quotes from Aristotle's Poetics to camouflage his soft porn with hard philosophy.

"We are already friends, Rafa. I know the real you and you know the real me, right? We don't have to be shallow and fake and needy like the rest of the narcissists in social media. Trust me, there are no real persons on Insta. Literally. For realz." This is from Pia. And guess what? I can't even answer that. Like really, I can't even...

"Lurve. Why be my follower when you are a born leader? I am not going to insult your awesomeness by having you as one of my legion of drooling fans." This is from Mitzi. And yes, legion of drooling fans is right. She can poison her followers with Kool-Aid and they would drink it in her honor. And you know what else is right? Legion of fapping fans. She can sell a fifteen-seconder vid of her touching herself and they would buy it in her honor. Nothing's free from this free spirit.

Compared to all of them, I just cannot market myself.

Because all I have is a real life.

And nothing kills Insta more than real life.

So there.

To Basti and Vicente, Pia and Mitzi, I am the one who is dead.

I am the one who is canceled.

I am the one who is a ghost.

All because of this shit called self-marketing.

Chapter Sixteen

S elf-authorship.
    This is it, my lurves. The simplest explaaaaaaaaaaaay as to why I keep blowing Rafa off every single time he reminds me about his fucking follower request on Insta.

I know. I know.

No matter how sus this sounds, this has nothing to do with him being my ex-BAE. Or that I was the one who dumped him. Or that he is still totes in lurve with moi after all this time.

This has everything to do with how Rafa just cannot market himself.

And why is that, my lurves?

Because Rafa just cannot author his very own story even if he fucking tries.

So how can you market yourself today if you don't have a story?

While he may believe that he has a story IRL, Rafa has zero stories on Insta, which, as we all know my lurves, is where it's really at.

And this is precisely why Rafa does not have a presence.

Which, in turn, is why he is canceled.

And so, he is a ghost.

I know. I know.
I will have to explain this self-authorship thing.
And why it is everything to my story.
Why it is the only thing to my story.
So here goes.
Take my OnlyFans.
You're a fan, right my lurves?
And if you're not, here's a shameless self-promotion. Why don't you haul your beautiful ass over to that site and become my fan? It's only $49.99 a month and you get a 15% discount with the code FRIDAY15! Yep, include that exclam. But this expires by midnight, so don't you waste another second thinking about it.
Anyhoo.
OnlyFans is a social media site where over a million content creators like me provide exclusive content to over 100 million subscribers who are appreciative patrons of hyper-curated videos and photos.
I know. I know.
That shit needs to be translated.
And here it is: OnlyFans is a social media site where over a million strippers like moi provide homemade porn to over 100 million pervs who masturbate to personalized vids and snaps according to their fetishes and perversions.
Now, here comes the humblebrag.
I am raking in the moolah via my OnlyFans.
I am leaving it at that because we, the wealthy class, have rules, my lurves. And the very first rule is that we never talk about wealth, instead, we just manage that wealth. Money talks, wealth keeps quiet. So, you will just have to trust me when I say that a serious amount of dough is being handed over

by my fans who are fapping to my homemade porn, ooops, excusez-moi, exclusive content, every single day.

The idea here is that my presence in this internet of things did not magically appear. Contrary to popular belief, my birthing as an—fuck this word—influencer, did not involve the mythical unicorn.

To mean: the rumors of my origin story have been greatly exaggerated.

Yep, my lurves, that exaggeration has been authored by none other than me.

See?

Self-authorship.

Here's a throwback Thursday to that time when it all began.

It was, literally, a Thursday, and, swear to gods, hope to die, it began with an iMessage and not a Twitter post. To use @Pia's words, "for realz."

That Thursday a few years ago, that adorable little slut decided to join the Miss Philippines, that once-a-year beauty pageant that is the unofficial official sport of La Fédération.

"Just to get it out of my system," she iMessaged me.

The timing was a bit sus, but who am I to get in the way of her ambition of debasing herself onstage, live on national TV and immortalizing this stupidity on YouTube? If wearing a crown and cradling a scepter while fully dressed in an evening gown after seeking validation from a dozen has-beens is her way of displaying her beauty, who am I to disagree?

But that timing, though.

When I say that the timing is a bit sus, what I mean is that @Pia decided to fulfill her dream of being a beauty titlist the very same year my parents FedExed my ass one way to Switzerland so that I would not witness the protracted cold war that was happening between the two of them. As if I did not know that they both want to completely destroy their marriage so that they both can continue having extramarital affairs. They are fucking cliches, the both of them. Gio was boning his secretary while 'Gette was sucking the cock of her best friend's husband. But whatevs. I'm not even gonna name names to protect the guilty. For the purpose of this story, I'll just call her Tessa Estrella and Tito Gil Castillo. Sorry, not sorry, Tita Virgie. You should have learned how to give a proper blowie. The technique is how to deploy just the right amount of teeth at just the right second.

Anyhoo.

That year, I was holed up at Lausanne, Switzerland, enrolled in the latest iteration of Château Mont-Choisi, once a finishing school for ladies, but now, while still exclusive for those biologically born with a vag, prides itself as a liberal arts college. Because, feminism. After a change in name, a working website, a two thousand percent increase of the matriculation and boarding fees, the antiquated school is now a modern college teaching us moneyed mademoiselles *two things and two things only. One: how to be a trophy wife. Two: how to speak and read and write the French language. See? How liberal is that? How liberating is that? Specially if you learn, as I have, how to give a proper blowie.*

So. While I was learning the genders of the thousand spoons and forks in a formal dining setting and swirling Chablis in my palette to pinpoint its most dominant bouquet, I get an iMessage.

"I'm totes taking home this year's bling," @Pia wrote. "For realz."

Now, I have to fess up, my lurves. I never doubted that she would be crowned Miss Philippines. In fact, she was already halfway there on the runway, doing the walk and the wave, the pirouette and the pose, the smile and the spiel. All that was needed during that time was a formal announcement. @Pia had already won.

I felt all this because that adorable little slut had already eliminated her fiercest competeeesh before the beauty pageant even began.

And that would be moi, *who else?*

So. Like any proper lady, I offered my congratulations in advance and told her to reach out if I could be of any help. Any help at all. She said her thanks and wished me luck, too. In my getting an education. And then I forgot all about it.

That is, until three things happened. One: a volcano in Iceland erupted. Two: this in turn, fucked up the schedule of the World Economic Forum making the rescheduled dates coincide with our semestral break. And three: back home, the cold war escalated to the point that money—money! ICB!—is now involved, with Gio cutting all of 'Gette's credit cards, the very same ones that my own plastics are anchored on. He also took her off the board of a gazillion charities and cut off her access to both The Manila Yacht Club and The Manila Polo Club. This is how civilized couples fight, my lurves, nothing verbal, nothing physical, it's all financial. Money is where the real power lies and if you use it as a weapon, you win the war quickly and quietly.

Yep, with my plastics now useless, I am broke as fuck while stuck in a foreign country.

And so, what is a Manila barrio lass on the way to becoming a Parisian mademoiselle *with zero Swiss francs to do?*

Head to Davos, of course!

Now, my lurves, here's another secret in the biz. There are only things worth going to if you are a mademoiselle *in waiting who needs a serious amount of liquid assets. One: the Cannes Advertising Festival AKA the Festival of Creativity in France. This is a worldwide junket of wannabe artists, writers, and filmmakers who just wanna smooch with the real powerbroker nowadays who are none other than the Silicon Valley fuckers. This "festival" is actually quite sad, seeing underage hookers with more culture than the advertising "creatives," but serious money could be had aside from the free snow if you know which chartered yacht you need to go to. Pro tip: it's FB or Google, never Ogilvy or McCann. Always bet on the tech companies and never on the ad agencies. Two: the World Economic Forum in Switzerland. This is one big circle jerk of politicians from all corners of the globe wherein they attempt to market themselves as the next thought leader who will save not just democracy as a whole but humanity as a race. This, while competing as to who could Hoover grade A coke the fastest. Just like that shit in Cannes, the Silicon Valley fuckers run this show although these moneyed little fuckers let the politicians pretend they are the ones in charge of world affairs and the welfare of the children of the future. If the advertising festival is sad, this Davos thing is quite cute. That one time I was there —swear to gods, hope to die, it was only that one time I was broke—I witnessed Bill Gates utter just a single word onstage that got him a standing ovation from democratic leaders and fascist dictators alike. "Mosquito," said the billionaire. He didn't even have a PowerPoint slide.*

I know. I know.

This getting to be quite a throwback. But this is my origin story so stick with me.

I was in Davos with a few of my fellow mademoiselles. *As one of the future wives or mistresses of the heads of states of first world countries, C-Suites of multinationals and conglomerates, and agented athletes of premiere leagues, I was wearing an open-back Givenchy gown paid for by my date for a gala dinner when inspiration struck.*

Pics or didn't happen, correct, my lurves?

And so, I ask my date—Al Gebra or Al Pombra from the House of Saud who is in Davos as the Head of Transportation of the Great Kingdom currently tasked to present the mind-blowing idea that the women in that part of the Middle East will soon be permitted by the King to drive cars unaccompanied by a man—to snap a pic of my OOTD.

And then I mentioned on my Twitter post @Pia who, it just so happens, is on the evening gown portion of the Miss

Philippines beauty pageant. My post was geotagged obvs, and had three appropriate hashtags.

And the rest, as they say, is herstory.

And just how did self-authorship come into play?

Well, my lurves, capitalizing on the accident of that one viral tweet, I authored a persona who competed against the crowd favorite of that year's Miss Philippines from halfway across this green Earth and gave her a run for her prize money.

Mitzi, the free spirit who can parle en Francais *and is on a first-name basis with Wall Street traders and third-world tyrants, is born. Some say that my birthplace was on that yacht, no, not something chartered but actually owned and named after* moi *anchored somewhere in the Aegean Sea where I hang out with Al Falfa after the conference, but I was really birthed on a red carpet in Davos.*

Mitziztahs, the fan community whose loyalty borders on them being zealots and extremists, soon followed.

And so, with very little effort, the manufactured rivalry between @Pia and me flourished, fueled by none other than our scripted nastiness towards each. We created one viral post after another like a bizarre love team whose awesomeness just couldn't be contained. The more we trashed each other, the more we trended. The outrage machine that is Twitter did its work, gathering us more fans, rewarding us with even more fame, and most important, showering us with lavish funds.

From the humble beginnings of the gay community defending me, the Mitziztahs mutated into a different animal altogether bent on championing everything Mitzi that even Twitter is no longer enough to handle the demand. The logical progression is to diversify and keep coming up with the supply.

And as my fanbase grew, so did my self-authorship.

Enter this free spirit reborn on Insta. A new life with unlimited filters. The nastiness and neediness in my fight with

@Pia *is replaced with the glam and the gloss of my very own show, one scheduled upload at a time. Fuck that adorable little slut that is @Pia. I have now become a brand with my very own aesthetic, targets, objectives, metrics, scores, partners, affiliates, KPIs, ROIs. And a rate card that prohibits any brand not serious enough to pay for my awesomeness in Benjamins. Swear to gods, hope to die, I can even afford to blow off Hollywood talent agencies and Silicon Valley influencer collectives. William Morris Endeavor? Fuck that! HypeHouse? Ditto. I don't need these parasites and never will.*

Why?

Because finally, my devoted fans and loyal followers whose demographic finally broke through the confines of the gay community, became my paying public.

Officially, I became an—fuck this word—influencer.

So, what else do I have to do but monetize my awesomeness?

I know you all follow me on my Insta, my lurves. So, you all know how my diversification from Insta to vlogging was seamless. And how fashion styling just happened, all the while maintaining my brand equity of being a free spirit.

A free spirit who now is no longer just being paid in flattery by my ever-growing fanbase but also in serious moolah by upmarket brands. My highly curated lifestyle became a highly lucrative business. Especially on my OnlyFans.

With every post, every heart, every share, every fucking thing that happens on my socials, I can hear a very loud kaching!

From just a single tweet, I was able to create living, breathing, and—this is très *important—an income-generating content.*

See?

Self-authorship.

And now that I have explained all this, my lurves, it's time for the next part of my story.

Chapter Seventeen

The next part of our story begins with Vicente joining us on the sofa.

He squeezes himself in between Mitzi and Pia.

Then he says something to no one.

"Everyone. Vicente wants to know what's happening tonight."

Basti shuts the door of his penthouse, locks it, and double-locks it.

He then walks over to the living room and sits down on one of the egg chairs facing us.

A second of silence engulfs the room.

Then Basti utters a single sentence.

"We are gathered here tonight for The Summoning."

I shit you not, that's what Basti says.

We are gathered here tonight for The Summoning.

You can almost see the capital T and the capital S of these two words.

The.

Summoning.
The Summoning.
The Summoning!
Like a classic novel by Stephen King. Or a title of a direct-to-video B movie starring Nicholas Cage.

Through the floor-to-ceiling glass window, I see a sliver of lightning forking down or it could just be one of the neon signs peppering the high-rise office building giving up the ghost. There's a faint boom that could be crack of thunder or a gunshot from somewhere in the city.

The Summoning!

Of course, none of us thinks that The Summoning would indeed be a summoning.

This is Basti, after all, who, just last week, introduced us to *Cards Against Humanity*.

Have you ever played that game? It is, as the box says, a party game for horrible people. Full of awkward, no holds barred topics that you are supposed to discuss. Topics like "Asians Who Aren't Good at Math." Don't laugh. "An M. Night Shyamalan Twist." See? Or this. "How to Conceal a Boner." Get it?

Anyway, The Summoning is not that kind of game. Because it is not a game at all, although horrible shit does happen on this Friday night.

In the middle of texting or trolling or whatever the fuck she is doing, Pia, already looking bored, speaks.

"How do we play it?" Pia says.

"Simple," Basti says. "We say a prayer to the Dark Lord. Then He, in His infinite malevolence, sends an evil spirit to visit us. And, hopefully, hilarity will ensue."

"For realz? Are you sucking my dick, Basti?" Pia says. When Basti does not reply, she continues with, "Ohhheeemgeee! My head literally exploded just listening to this crap!"

As a punctuation to this outburst, Pia slaps Vicente's knee and rests her hand on it after giving it a squeeze.

A moment of silence follows.

I can hear Mitzi try very hard not to laugh. She starts gathering her stuff from the coffee table. iPhone, bag, a pack of Marl red, and a travel-size Johnson & Johnson baby powder.

Pia's boredom mutates into a barely disguised irritation and this is conveyed via a perfectly trimmed eyebrow rising very slowly. And who can blame her? I know that there are a million other things that she would rather be doing this Friday night. A million other dudes she would rather be *doing* this Friday night.

I keep my silence.

I look at Basti. Then at everyone.

Because to be honest, I am interested. Who would not be interested in summoning an evil spirit on a stormy Friday night?

Finally, Vicente speaks.

"Vicente thinks we should do it."

And so, of course...

Chapter Eighteen

O
f course, it is @Vicente.

Of all the people in the room this stormy Friday night, the lousy little retard @Vicente is the one who speaks that we all should do it.

"Vicente thinks we should do it."

Yes, my lurves, such innocent words spoken, as per yoozh, in the third.

I am so ready to pack up and have myself a proper Friday.

I have even gathered my things from the table and have stood up.

I'm sure Rafa would go with me the second I call out his name. You know, that thing with the question mark that makes him real hard, real fast.

Maybe even @Pia might also go as she is looking so bored already that I might as well put her out of her misery by inviting her, too.

That is, until @Basti mentions what he is cooking up this Friday.

"We are gathered here tonight for The Summoning."

Swear to gods, hope to die, those are the very same words that @Basti utters.

The.

Summoning.

The Summoning.

The Summoning!

I nearly burst out laughing as it is totes magotes, sounding like a blatant rip off of that Reddit shit that trended a million years ago, The Fappening. Remember that, my lurves?

The Fappening is this thing that unleashed a ton of Hollywood celebs' nudes into the wild, exposing the shaved ho-ha of the Who's Ho for all the pervs on Reddit to fap to their dicks' content. Starting from an anonymous drop of nudes, The Fappening became a hackathon. Then it morphed into a crowdsourcing game. The folder on Reddit continued collecting the snaps of starlets and athletes, singers and activists, and the files just kept growing like a fucking mutant monster. Curation gone wild. And yet, the Fappening kept on happening.

And yes, my lurves, the victims of The Fappening cried foul. Of course, they fucking did. They whined and bitched about it in the mainstream media, in their social media, and even on Reddit where it all began.

I have to fess up that while I found it to be funny AF, the complaining of these celebs and not the whole nudity thing. I'm sure that if it were to happen to me, I would totally lose my shit, too.

Because The Fappening occurred way before OnlyFans or Patreon. You know, the Before Times.

The Fappening democratized their nudes without them being marketed and monetized. L'horreur!

Anyhoo.

I'm guessing that @Basti has dug up some crap on Reddit and that The Summoning is one of those obscure shit that has yet to trend. It could be a game. It could be a show. It could *even be a fucking Norwegian heavy metal band that I have no plan of giving a listen to. I just couldn't be sure of anything when it comes to @Basti on any given Friday.*

Thankfully, the silly little heartbreaker explains what he is thinking.

According to @Basti, we are going to connect with @Satan Himself and He, in his Badassery, will send us one of His many followers and we will have ourselves a trending event. A viral event. Think of the hearts and the shares. The comments and the conversations.

At least that's the plan as I have heard it, reduced to less than 140 characters.

@Pia, at first bored, is now curious all of a sudden. The adorable little slut even does her fake outrage schtick which @Basti, ever the loyal BAE, dutifully ignores.

Moi? I'm ready to call it a night and just enjoy this Friday with my stash of snow.

And then @Vicente speaks in the third.

"Vicente thinks we should do it."

@Basti obliges.

Chapter Nineteen

And so, of course, Basti obliges.

He adjusts his egg chair so that he is smack in the middle of our little formation on the white modular sofa. He has a full view of us, and us, of him. The arc lamp shines directly down on his head, showering him with brightness like one of Lola's *santitos y santitas*.

He raises both his hands and grabs Pia on his right, mine on his left, and everyone gets the idea.

Before we could close our eyes and bow our heads, I see Pia break her hold to do the sign of the cross. Either out of instinct with her being from a Catholic school and all, or, who knows, maybe she is just the religious type.

"That's not how we begin a prayer to the Dark Lord," Basti says. "You have to uncross yourself."

What follows is a very heated discussion about the mechanics of uncrossing one's self. And whether Pia should be the only one to uncross herself.

To move things forward, we all uncross ourselves.

We do an inverted cross where the left to right part is done on the lower portion of the abdomen.

I see Vicente adjust his balls halfway through and I file

the idea in case I get the "How to Conceal a Boner" in our next *Cards Against Humanity* game.

Once we are all holding hands again and our heads are bowed with our eyes closed, Basti says a prayer.

———

The prayer is in Latin.

Maybe.

Or Aramaic.

Or Sumerian.

It sounded like what my Lolo would call a dead language.

Or.

It could be something out of *The Lord of the Rings.* Maybe even *Harry Potter.* Or *Game of Thrones.*

Or.

It could be something that Basti has just made up that very moment.

But.

But...

But!

Deep in my guts I think it is in Latin.

That dead language.

I know a thing or two about dead languages because I grew up in a very religious household. The kind where there is a *novena* at promptly six in the evening. The kind where you bend your right knee when you do the sign of the cross inside a church. The kind where you always eat the body of Christ and drink His blood every time you celebrate mass.

And why is this, you may ask?

Well, my Lolo is the former *Arsobispo de Manila.*

But patience. I will explain that shit later.

Back to Basti's prayer.

Though it sounded Latin, I could not be sure if I have ever heard a prayer like that.

It's because the storm finally comes as soon as Basti starts uttering his prayer and some of his words are drowned out, snatched away before I could catch them.

Thunder. Lighting. Very, very fright'ning.

I open my eyes.

Everyone is still bowed with their eyes wide shut and I look around as Basti continues muttering these foreign words and phrases that are mostly getting lost in the gathering storm.

The power is cut for a second and total darkness descends.

I see bolts of lightning cracking up the night sky. I swear that the streaks of brilliance seem to come from somewhere down below. Same with the deafening boom that follows. It sounded like hell has opened up and some majestic power is launching an assault heavenwards.

Thunder. Lighting. Very, very fright'ning.

Momentary blindness that echoes in my retinas followed by the sound of crashing thunder that reverberates inside my ears.

Thunder. Lighting. Very, very fright'ning.

An unnerving sight. A guttural sound.

When the power returns, my eyes take a moment to adjust. I feel that the room, despite the arc lamp and the overhead track lights now working again, seems a bit darker than before.

Hard rain pelts down on the penthouse, liquid bullets pounding the floor-to-ceiling glass window so that the outside world is rendered as one blurry vista.

A bolt of lightning shoots down from the heavens followed by a rumble of thunder that shakes my bones.

And also deflates my boner.

Basti lets go of our hands and this is when I notice that his prayer has ended.

Only then did I know that the words that Basti has just offered to the Dark Lord are even more frightening than the thunder and the lightning and the tropical storm that is now raging.

And these, if my mind could be trusted, are the very same words that Basti has just uttered for The Summoning.

GIGANTVM PENISIVM.

SATANVM SPIRITVM.

SACRIFICIVM VIRGINVM.

BROKENVM HYMENVM.

SVMMONVM DAEMONIVM.

Chapter Twenty

ABSVRDVM PASSWORDVM.
PORTALVM SECRETVM.
ACCESSVM INFERNVM.
ESCAPVM DAEMONIVM.
MORTALVM POSSESSVM.

These are not @Basti's words.

These, my lurves, are my take on them.

I am not going to take a chance and repeat the very same words that @Basti utters in his prayer because, swear to gods, hope to die, the fucker really does The Summoning.

Understand that this is my story. And I am doing this for your protection.

Trust me on this, my lurves.

I know. I know. That was a cop-out. I am doing this to protect myself and myself only. Because I am both innocent and guilty. Then again, aren't we all?

Anyhoo.

@Basti's prayer is a fucking password that is so crypto it is absurd as fuck.

But it works.

His incantation, this combineeesh of fucking weirdness

that he surely just made up, is accepted on his first attempt, eliminating the need for the two-auth process without activating a fire alarm.

And just what does this absurd password do, my lurves?

Well, it only opens hell itself.

@Basti fucking hacks the underworld, this silly little heartbreaker whom I would never peg as a Satan worshipper, gets through the highly resilient firewall and tears asunder all the security protocols of that bottomless pit, rewriting a badly written code like the leet that he is and unlocks a fiery backdoor that only Beelzebub, the webmaster of Gehenna, has access to. Again, a shoutout to Sister Heidi.

Of course, @Basti calls it a prayer and we even do an inversion of the sign of the cross with our eyes closed and our heads bowed and our hands linked. With @Pia, the adorable little slut, being the first to do it, the proper sign of the cross that @Basti hastily corrects. And who can fault her when @Pia knows nothing about praying, much more to the Dark Lord? Kneeling in front of a papa on the other hand...

Anyhoo.

A prayer or a password spoken in a language that could either be long dead or a working code, same diff.

We're in.

Ooooops. Strike that, my lurves.

@Basti lets something in.

Or rather, he—l'horreur!—invites someone in.

As soon as @Basti says these words, I open my eyes.

Only to find that everything is dark. Deep and dark like the whole place is locked on the M1 filter and loaded with a fucking vignette and oversaturated in grayness.

The edges of my vision are a bit blurred and everything is muffled.

I know. I know.

It could just be the storm that is now upon us, rain and wind and what have you, but there is something surreal that I just cannot pin down what the fuck it is like a hashtag so unsticky that I cannot remember it.

I look at everyone.

@Basti is smiling to himself, eyes also scanning the room, squinting to adjust in the dark that has descended. I read, on his face, not satisfaction but curiosity. Like he is not sure whether his prayer worked. Or, if it did, what are the implicaaays?

Rafa is no longer a lost puppy but a frightened one. He is also taking everything in, the darkened room, the pounding storm, but his face is a canvas of worry. No, not worry but fear. No, not fear but terror. Pure, unadulterated terror. Swear to gods, hope to die, I even see him tremble. Poor Rafa!

@Pia is catatonic. One of her hands is still holding @Vicente's but she is unmoving, her eyes looking at nothing at all. Her chest is moving very slowly as she breathes in and out, but that's all there is to her. Like she is there with us, but not really. Her stillness layers the penthouse with another kind of silence.

***

And then @Vicente speaks.

Chapter Twenty-One

And then Vicente speaks.

"By your mandate, through the grace of the Almighty, I stand here today in the traditional ritual of the assumption of the Presidency. By your mandate, once again you have demonstrated the vitality of our democracy by the peaceful transference of governmental authority. It is but fitting and proper that this traditional ritual be undertaken on this sacred ground. For sixty-nine years ago today, a young patriot and prophet of our race fell upon this beloved soil. He fell from a tyrant's bullet and out of the martyr's blood that flowed copiously there sprang a new nation."

All of us shout all at once.

"Vicente!?"

But he continues with his speech, if you can call that shit a speech, which is even more confusing than Basti's fucked up Latin.

"This is your dream and mine. By your choice you have committed yourselves to it. Come then, let us march together towards the dream of greatness."

"Vicente?" We all ask again.

And here's the thing that removes all doubt that indeed, an evil fucking spirit was summoned.

"Vicente who?" Vicente replies.

"You're Vicente. Literally. For realz," Pia says, moving a couple of inches away from him.

"Men..." Basti says, maybe the very first time ever in his life that he really meant not finishing his sentence.

"Stop licking my balls, Vicente," Mitzi says.

"I'm not Vicente," Vicente says. Note that he is no longer speaking in the third person like a fucking retard.

"So, you who are you?" I ask him.

And fuck as fuck, Vicente answers.

"What you've just heard was The Mandate for Greatness and my name is Ferdinand Emmanuel Edralin Marcos, Sr.!"

Chapter Twenty-Two

The name is Ferdinand Emmanuel Edralin Marcos, Sr. And he is babbling something or other about a mandate for awesomeness.

Whoever the fuck it is that @Basti has summoned by praying to the Dark Lord is now possessing that lousy little retard @Vicente.

It's like a Fortnite crossover skin but inside out: it is still the skin of @Vicente but someone is in it.

Or an out-of-body experience but in reverse: someone has traveled into @Vicente's body and giving us an experience.

Even an augmented reality experience: but in real life and in fucking 3D with no need for those shitty goggles.

A badly written ep of that TV show Black Mirror but with analog tech: praying to His Malevolence, how analog is that?

And the irony is not lost on me either, my lurves.

For among the five of us, it is @Vicente himself, the early adapter of all things emerging tech that was accessed.

I know, I know.

The word is possessed.

It's the weirdest shit I have ever seen on a Friday, and

believe me, my lurves, I have seen a lot of weird shit on a lot of Fridays.

So.

Who the fuck is this Ferdinand?

The first thing we do, all of us behaving like one sentient organism but with different bodies and voices, is to shout all at once.

"Vicente?"

"Vicente who?" @Vicente replies.

And it is at this very moment that I know that @Vicente has been rewired. Corrupted. Hijacked. A worm is unleashing havoc into his operating system doing its own reprog as he speaks.

And note, my lurves, that he is no longer speaking in the third.

@Vicente has been hacked.

This Friday, with the storm lashing outside the floor-to-ceiling window with all the fury in the world, is starting to get interesting.

And then another power outage occurs.

Darkness falls.

Chapter Twenty-Three

Another power outage enshrouds the penthouse in total darkness. Something solid that ravages not just my vision but my sanity as well. This fucking storm. On this fucking Friday.

I'm sure everyone is being fucked the same way. I can feel that breaths are held, pulses are quickened, marrows are chilled.

Lightning comes. Of course, it does. Brighter, bigger, and more blinding than before. A second, an eternity, that freezes us all. Thunder follows. Somebody might have shrieked or Vicente must have laughed out loud or it could have just been my very own heart exploding but the sonic boom warps everything.

When the power returns, everything inside the apartment seems darker. *Is* darker. Even the arc lamp shining down on Basti.

"Ferdinand who?" I ask everyone.

No one replies. Everyone is silent as the dead.

"Basti? Do you know who this Ferdinand is? Mitzi? Pia?" I make a roll call just to be sure that not one of us really knows who the fuck this Ferdinand is.

The name does not ring any bell.

"K," Mitzi says. "We are going to crowdsource this shit to Twitter."

I've already said this. But for the sake of this narrative, I will say it again.

Mitzi has millions of followers on her social media. I shit you not. Millions.

Facebook, Instagram, Twitter, TikTok, YouTube, Only-Fans, and whatever other shit is out there. Followers, communities, fans, public, whatever you may call them, Mitzi has them.

"Hey...woke peeps," Mitzi says, her agile fingers gliding on the sleek surface of her iPhone. "Anybody...know...Ferdinand... Emmanuel...Edralin...Marcos? Question...mark. Claiming...to...be...our...president. Exclam, question mark, exclam."

The sent chime comes, loud and disturbing in the silence of the penthouse.

I turn to Vicente.

"You are Ferdinand who?" I ask.

But instead of answering, Vicente, or whoever the fuck that Ferdinand is, gets up from the sofa and shoves Basti away from his egg chair so that he gets the prime spot in the living room, the arc light framing his being, all the more to get our undivided attention.

And this is when shit starts to happen.

Vicente speaks once more.

"Listen very carefully for I will not say this again.

"The name is Ferdinand Emmanuel Edralin Marcos, Sr., and I am going to lead us to greater heights you would never have thought possible. All you have to do is to follow me and together we can achieve my vision of building a great republic."

It is at this point that Pia, looking bitchier than her usual self, speaks.

"Do you mind reducing that awesome speech, Mr. Ferdinand, Sir, to one hundred and forty characters?"

Before Vicente, or that Ferdinand, can answer, Pia fires again.

"And would that awesome vision of yours somewhat involve any alcohol on the horizon? And I have nothing against doing a bit of blow."

Now, let me remind you that our story is happening on a Friday with neither a drop of alcohol nor a gram of cocaine in our systems and all of us are really thirsty as fuck.

Pia is just being Pia and not someone trying to be funny.

Vicente answers.

"That would be President Marcos, to you, Meldy. But yes, of course, my dear Meldy. Why is that even a question? Alcohol! Cocaine! Let us properly celebrate my ascent into the highest seat of the Republic!"

So, Vicente heads over to the bar and opens the fridge. He liberates a bottle of a Moët and grabs five flutes, cradling their long stems in between his fingers.

Meanwhile, Mitzi takes out an AmEx platinum credit card from her bag and a travel-size bottle of Johnson & Johnson's baby powder. Nice touch, I must say. Hypoallergenic cocaine. Because the baby is now a junkie. With the manual dexterity of a surgeon doing brain surgery, she cuts five straight lines of the Peruvian marching powder smack on the center table.

Heading back to the sofa, Vicente addresses Pia.

"Meldy, my love. One hundred and forty characters cannot capture my vision, can't you see? After this presidency is a dictatorship. And after that dictatorship is a monarchy. Yes! My dear Meldy! We are going to rename the Philippines

as Maharlika! Crown ourselves as monarchs! Power in perpe-
tuity! I shall be your King Ferdinand and you shall be my
Queen Imelda!"

Pia takes in what Vicente, or that Ferdinand, is saying and
beams. Her face lights up with a wattage that brightens the
room more than the dimming arc lamp and the overhead halo-
gens and the oversized neons outside the window. Or it could
just be from the coke that she has just Hoovered with her left
nostril. Not a single granule is wasted.

I know this because I had my eyes on her the whole time
so that I could catch a glimpse of her milkers as she bent
down. And yes, if you're curious, I get rewarded with a
glimpse of a purple-pinkish nipple I have yet to defile trying to
break free from her see-through bra. I do a mental screenshot
of her boobs and save it in my spank bank.

Vicente distributes the glasses, bubbling to the brim with
the champagne. Basti's very expensive champagne.

He raises his hand and motions for us to follow him.
Fucking Vicente. That retard.

"A toast to us Filipinos! To our resilient nation! To our
bright future!"

Chapter Twenty-Four

The future is looking very bright indeed.

And this, despite @Vicente being hacked, the power getting erratic as fuck, and the storm still gathering strength and unleashing its unbridled fury across the metropolis.

Because, snow.

And, the Moët.

Credit where credit is due, but it is that adorable little slut @Pia who started this partaaay on this stormy Friday.

So.

@Vicente, who is now Ferdinand, dethrones @Basti from his place on the egg chair and proclaims himself as Ferdinand Emmanuel Edralin Marcos, Sr., a name that is longer than moi by one word via that suffix.

This fucker is a Sr.

And he is mumbling something about building a strong presence in the aether. And that he is enlisting me in this project. All that I have to do? Be his fan and follower.

As fucking if.

@Pia suggests that we have a drink, and @Vicente, who is now Ferdinand, obliges.

I bring out my stash and cut us all a line. It's the least I could do, share the wealth of nations in our little Earth, and make my humble contribution to this Friday that is starting to get really sick. Plus, it's just the etiquette in polite society that the one who's holding socializes the snow.

It is hypoallergenic heaven contained in a 50g baby powder plastic bottle that I evenly divide using my platinum AmEx. Each under his own fig tree, my brother's keeper, and all that Biblical shit that Sister Heidi has taught us. Basically, be nice. Specially if you have a stash.

I do my line using a rolled-up newly minted Benjamin just to be on brand.

And gods know that I needed to get pumped real hard. What with @Vicente, who is now Ferdinand, calling @Pia "my dear Meldy."

Who the fuck?

And not only that, my lurves!

@Vicente, who is now Ferdinand, wants to crown @Pia as his one and only BAE! Like a fucking queen or something. And he promises that they are going to dominate the world like a power couple and internet superstars!

What the fuck?

And get this, my lurves, @Pia is really digging this thing, whatever this is. The adorable little slut is getting moist, basking in the attention that she is getting from that lousy little retard @Vicente, who is now Ferdinand, forgetting that her BAE, @Basti, is right there beside her.

Meldy.

Ferdinand.

And this Ferdinand is mumbling that I should follow him.

Well, this Ferdinand will be schooled that I did not become an—fuck this world—influencer by following a single soul. Yep, my lurves, I never follow anyone and never will. Go ahead and check out my profile. That's right. Zero followers on all accounts. See?

All of us are clueless AF as to who this Ferdinand is, and I decide that is it time for a proper WHOIS query. Via Twitter, of course. Time to enlist the help of that ever-dependable outrage machine. With just a single tweet, I know I can do my own discovery phase and dox this Ferdinand like he has never been doxed before.

I open my iPhone and get to work.

"Hey woke peeps. Anybody know Ferdinand Emmanuel Edralin Marcos, Sr.,? Claiming to be our president!?!"

The tweet is sent into the aether and I go back to the party.

I see that while the adorable little slut has forgotten the existence of @Basti, she has not forgotten the existence of the snow on the table. @Pia vacuums her line in one fluid motion, clean as a fucking whistle like the veteran junkie that she is. She recognizes quality shit when she sees one and she does not let a single granule go to waste.

I see Rafa take a mental screenshot of her girls as she bends down, edits it, labels it, and then files it inside one of the many porn folders of his filthy mind. The sight is so sad knowing that @Pia just asked him about his life just minutes earlier. Poor Rafa!

Anyhoo.

We started doing the snow and sipping the champagne.

The bottle of Moët still has another round for the five of us as @Vicente, who is now Ferdinand, sets it on the table. He continues to call @Pia as his Meldy.

As I ride the adrenaline that only high-grade cocaine can provide, it hits me.

That everything is funny as fuck.

Chapter Twenty-Five

Now that is really funny.

Pia getting baptized as Meldy.

Who the fuck is Meldy?

I look at Pia and I see that she is also ignorant as to who this Meldy is. But I get the sense that she is enjoying the attention from Vicente, or that Ferdinand.

Pia whips out her iPhone and snaps about a dozen selfies with Vicente, or that Ferdinand, who obliges, forgetting that the rest of us are still in the room. She uploads whatever needs uploading. Updates whatever it is that needs updating. Feeds whatever needs feeding. And yes, I most certainly mean her ego as well.

iPhones, except mine of course, vibrate and ping with alerts. All of us ignore them. Instead, we snort the coke and drink the champagne and do our best to make this Friday a fucking Friday.

Ah, the Moët. A fitting drink on this dark and stormy night despite the lunatic possessing Vicente.

A mandate for greatness, my ass. As incomprehensible as Basti's GIGANTVM PENISIVM.

I reach for the bottle of bubbly and help myself to a second pour.

And this is when I hear Vicente, or that Ferdinand, speak.

"Please do the honor of pouring your leader another."

What the fuck?

Your leader?

Seriously?

So, what I do is pour everyone else first, making sure to refill their glasses until they overflow, intentionally wasting precious liquid with a vintage that is older than all of us in the penthouse.

And then I pour the remaining drop, literally—did I use that term right, literally?—to "my leader."

Vicente, or that Ferdinand, speaks again.

"That kind of insolence will not be tolerated in my regime, boy!"

And as he is uttering these words, the retard actually slaps me. He transfers his flute to his left hand and then hits me with his right, squarely landing on my left cheek so that I could feel my molars and wisdom teeth rearrange themselves in alphabetical order.

I am too stunned to hit back.

Plus, I am more concerned about my drink going to waste.

So, after downing my second glass, I answer Vicente, that retard, or whoever the fuck that Ferdinand, is.

"This has gone far enough," I say calmly. "You need to fucking chill Vicente or whoever the fuck you are, before things go beyond your control."

I see Basti nod his agreement.

Both Mitzi and Pia seem lost, even stopping from tinkering with their iPhones. Like on the one hand, they find what is happening to be super weird, but on the other, they want this weirdness to continue. That this, whatever the fuck this is, is 'Grammable. Sharable. Likable. This might even trend.

And by continue, I mean, both of them want to see me hit Vicente back.

Yes, these are the kinds of ladies I am attracted to. Don't judge, please.

And guess what?

I did get to hit that retard back.

But I don't wanna get ahead of our story.

Now, after I recover my senses, things take a turn for the worse. Of fucking course, it did.

The room vibrates from the wind outside.

And also from Mitzi's phone as her tweet starts to generate responses, retweets, and hearts.

"Anybody recognize who the fuck this Ferdinand is?" I ask.

Mitzi scrolls down her feed and reads the replies.

"Nope, nope, nope. The who?! LOL! Is he cute? Nope. Ferdinand who? Is he hot? Nope. Send me a pic. Send me your pussy pic. Gimme a squirt vid. Nope. Who? Never heard. Who that?"

I guess the rest of the world is as clueless as we are that night. Not a single woke fuck knows this Ferdinand.

And then Vicente, or that Ferdinand, speaks again.

"You have to understand that this is just politics. The art of the possible. And I need your help to make my vision become possible.

"As I have said before, all you have to do is follow me.

"There's a lot to be done but first, we need to secure some funding.

"For infrastructure. For arts and culture. For nation building.

"I need all your money so we can make all this possible."

Mitzi downs her second glass of the Moët and faces Vicente.

"Excuse me?" Mitzi says. "What the fuck are you saying? I know you are fucking high from this high-grade snow, but what the fuck?!"

Vicente, or that Ferdinand, replies.

"I think I have made it clear as day. I need all your money. This great republic of ours will not build itself."

And just like that, Vicente actually starts rummaging Mitzi's stuff.

He opens her bag and takes out her wallet and plunders her cash.

Mitzi, too shocked by this dick move, isn't even able to unleash a comeback.

All of her cash—newly-minted US D plus unsorted crumpled bills like any self-respecting dude would have, including a few coins—are forcibly taken from her. There are maybe a dozen signed checks, too.

And it is quite a handful of cash, believe you me.

Especially that thick wad of US D, all in hundreds, crisp and clean like newly laundered linen. This is at the bottom of her bag, wrapped in a sort of contract, maybe a non-disclosure or a non-compete.

And why, you may ask, is Mitzi carrying that kind of cash this Friday night?

Well, maybe her latest fashion show is on a *kaliwaan*

basis. Maybe she's just withdrawn some spending money from her latest royalty generated by her performance art on OnlyFans. Maybe her family business just cut her this quarter's dividends. All very lucrative, I must add.

Especially that family business of hers.

But now, all these moolah are being grabbed by Vicente, by that Ferdinand, as he once again speaks.

"This will go into the Marcos highway. Imagine the rest of the islands with working roads and bridges and seaports and airports. Commerce, education, and modernization will soon follow. All that and more, will start with this tax."

Vicente, or that Ferdinand, divides Mitzi's money into two and pockets both amounts.

And then he continues.

"Now, half of these will go into my retirement fund. We all know that you can't beg money from the United States forever. And that mansion on Fifth Avenue does not come cheap. The Monets alone...the catered dinners...the jazz bands..."

And before I know it, it is now my turn to contribute to nation-building.

The fucking retard also fleeces me right there and then like he has every god-given right to.

He physically wrangles my money off my hands when I try to resist like he is a founding member of The Quiapo Joggers' Society.

What? Don't you tell me you haven't heard a thing or two about The Quiapo Joggers' Society?

They are the commonest of criminals! The low-life snatchers preying upon unsuspecting victims by the Quiapo churchyard and the underground walkway that is Ils-de-Tuls!

Compared to Mitzi's moolah, what Vicente, or that Ferdinand takes from me is but a pittance of course.

Only because I am not yet into the family business.

Okay.

At this point in our story, it might be best to explain what the fuck being in the family business means.

Simply put: it is getting paid by Daddy and Mommy doing whatever it is the fuck you want to do.

Which is basically staying out of their way so that Daddy and Mommy can continue making even more money.

Mitzi's family business is politics.

Her father is a Congressman or maybe a Senator, I don't really know as I have never voted. All I know is that his official salary is but mere loose change to all that the payolas and grease money and discretionary allowances that arrive like clockwork. So, imagine if you can, all the moolah she is raking in on top of her earnings from her internet hobbies. Then there's the fashion styling, too.

Pia's family business is in the media and entertainment industry.

Newspaper and magazines as well as TV and radio stations. All over the islands with a few outposts in select cities worldwide. They have enough foresight to pivot into new media, including an online newspaper with a paywall and a video-based news gathering outfit that syndicates stories to the usual news brokerages. Their shit is everywhere that it is practically a monopoly.

Basti's family business is real estate.

The usual formula. They buy what could be bought, hold on to it for a couple of years, and bid out the lease to developers for X number of years before they take everything back. They practically lord over the fucking country, IMHO. That joke about owning land as far as the eye can see is not a joke to Basti. They even have properties abroad if the whispers among the moneyed are to be believed.

Vicente's family business is banking and finance.

Their bank was the very first financial institution to seriously recognize and set up branches in the far-flung municipalities being ignored by the major players in the metropolis. It would soon turn out to be a very profitable venture as we only have one overrated capital city compared to thirteen flourishing regions. Like all things successful, this money-making machine ultimately ended up in select cities favored by OFWs. Abu Dhabi, Qatar, Dubai, Hong Kong, Singapore, even New York and LA, as well as London and Barcelona.

Me? Well, our family was previously into the salvation business.

My Lolo, as I have said, is the former *Arsobispo de Manila*, although only a very chosen few know about it. The tired family joke is that he succeeded in serving not just god and mammon but also Lola who was a very devout parishioner, may god rest her soul.

My father, their lovechild, was conceived inside a confessional during Friday the thirteenth—ha! Friday!, see?—and wanted to have nothing to do with being a priest, thank fucking god. Imagine if he answered his calling and was actually celibate. *Que horror!*

Today, my family is in the peacekeeping hardware business. We are purveyors of analog killing machines.

Yes, we are gunrunners.

My father imports guns and ammunitions and any other crap that would kill the fastest, the cleanest, and the easiest. Mostly, he supplies the Armed Forces of the Philippines and the New People's Army, although he maintains a very select roster of private clientele. Vetted individuals only who are discreet and willing to pay a premium price for top-of-the-line hardware from the United States, Austria, and Israel.

So, you might say that we are still in the salvation business, something whose profit I want to be part of, now that I plan to stop being a desk jockey and live the life of a woke. Or a BEA. Or even better, a woke BAE.

But as I haven't yet handed my fuck you letter to my boss, what I have in my pocket this Friday night is just a few bills. Beer money.

And guess what?

Even that loose change is taken away by Vicente, by that Ferdinand, too.

Chapter Twenty-Six

Everything is being taken away.
And this is not an exaggeraaay, my lurves.
Every fucking thing.

@Vicente, who is now Ferdinand, starts with my hard-earned money but I get the vibe that he is going to take a lot more. A whole fucking lot more before this Friday night is through.

But I don't want to do a jump cut on my story.

That would defeat its purpose and sabotage its lesson.

You remember my promise, right, my lurves?

There will be a lesson.

And so, before I go to that moolah grab that is currently in progress inside @Basti's living room, let me continue my story with that bitchslap that happens between two dudes.

@Pia, the adorable little slut, gets the idea of taking a selfie with that lousy little retard @Vicente, who is now Ferdinand. Because, Insta. And just like her joining the Miss Philippines beauty contest, who am I to stop her?

As *@Pia clicks the photos away, Rafa heads over to the table to refill his glass of the bubbly. @Basti's bubbly. The Moët. The fucking 1979 Moët & Chandon Epsrit du Siecle Brut.*

Before Rafa does the pour, @Vicente, who is now Ferdinand, tells him, no, commands him to pour "your leader first." Swear to gods, hope to die, @Vicente, who is now Ferdinand, refers to himself no longer in the third but as "your leader."

Well.

Rafa does the pour. To every one of us. But he makes sure that his leader gets refilled the last. With just a single drop.

This earns him a mighty bitchslap from @Vicente, who is now Ferdinand.

And it's a good and proper bitchslap, too.

Rafa is thrown off his center of gravity and loses his balance. Precious champagne is spilled. Righteous anger is aroused. And from moi, riotous laughter is suppressed. Because, manners. A dude slapping another, how funny is that? Although I keep this thought to myself and bottle my laughter in.

But here's one thing that sticks with me, my lurves. I saw a little bit of fight in Rafa. While he did not repay @Vicente, who is now Ferdinand, with a bitchslap plus interest and an extra charge for damages and attorney's fees, there is a major vibe that Rafa will not let this one go. That he is just bidding his time before he royally fucks "his leader."

Just then, my iPhone comes alive, screaming with pings and alerts and notifications like it too, was possessed AF. The wind and the storm and the rain have no game to the uproar that this moi machine is causing so that it could get my attention, its touch screen lighting up and its naked body vibrating like a newly juiced Lelo.

My question on Twitter is now answered.

And guess what, my lurves?

Not a single soul among my millions of fans and followers, my loyal patrons and my devoted public, knows who the fuck this Ferdinand is.

He is a fucking ghost.

I read aloud the replies to everyone just so we are all on the same page. The same blank page.

All confirmations that everyone, like the five of us in the living room, is as clueless as to who this Ferdinand is.

"Nope, nope, nope. The who?! Is he cute? Nope. Ferdinand who? Is he hot? Nope. Send me a pic. Send me your pussy pic. Gimme a squirt vid. Nope. Who? Never heard. Who that?"

While this is happening, @Vicente, who is now Ferdinand, is mumbling some shit about building his personal brand. His presence in the aether. And that, swear to gods, hope to die, he needs our help to achieve his vision. Of course, it involves following him, becoming his fan. Being his friend.

And not only that, my lurves, he also has this one ask: he needs some moolah. So that he can have the bandwidth that he needs for his go-live. Yep, no beta testing, straight to product launch. This Ferdinand is moving fast and breaking things like a fucking tech bro.

And whose moolah is he talking about, my lurves?

Moi, of course!

@Vicente, who is now Ferdinand, loots my bag and grabs my cash. Even found the Benjamins that I stashed at the bottom with my share of the snow. My hard-earned daily bread from a project that I only do on a Friday, my me day. Every single bill and every single check and even the spare change are liposuctioned off my bag. Not the Birkin, but my Friday bag that is the Herschel tote. This, as he continues mumbling something or other about taxes and retirement funds and Fifth Avenue mansions and catered dinners and jazz bands.

What the fuck?

Indeed, my lurves.

But wait, there's more to this methodical madness.

@Vicente, who is now Ferdinand, moves on to fleecing Rafa of all the money that is on his person.

Which is just pocket money compared to mine, but still. Thievery is thievery. Commandment number seven, right Sister Heidi? Every single crumpled cash, every single defaced coin is forcibly liberated from Rafa's pocket with the comedic movement of a bumbling burglar. Like Lupin with zero finesse. But who needs finesse when free money, no matter how small the amount, is to be had?

Now, my lurves, it's time to talk about Rafa's money.

Or his lack of.

Of all the beautiful people this stormy Friday night, Rafa is the only one among us who is not into the family business.

I know. I know.

Remember the rule: we the wealthy do not talk about wealth, all we do is just manage the wealth.

A corollary to this cardinal rule: we talk freely about other people's lack of wealth.

Oh, fuck yes, my lurves, we do. We do it a lot that it is now an unofficial official sport among ourselves, more than giving anonymous donations in the millions to charities, the environment, the church, political pawns, and communist rebels. Making fun of the have-nots is the original meme, something passed around the analog way. Via gossip, of course, the original information superhighway whose bandwidth is unlimited and runs faster than 5G. Like blockchain technology but old fucking school. Think of this: how fucking decentralized and democratized is gossip? Yep, that is a mental orgasm that I gave you right fucking there for free. You're welcome.

Anyhoo.

Back to Rafa's lack of money and his being out of the family business.

The former is the result of the latter,

Or, to put it another way, the latter is the cause of the former.

Cause and effect.

Stimulus and response.

Like self-authorship and presence.

Or self-marketing and profits.

Insta and fame.

OnlyFans and stardom.

Family business and unlimited moolah.

———

But Rafa, rather than go into the family business, his *family business*, decided to enslave himself in the corporate world and be a subservient monkey chained to a desk, cranking out profits for his overlords. It's sad AF, really.

Especially since I know that his family's business is one of the most lucrative industries on this green Earth.

And their business is: gunrunning.

Pimping guns to organizations and individuals alike.

Rafa's family is a part of the military-industrial complex, the only industry that rivals pharmaceuticals, both legal and illegal, in raking in the profits. His family imports guns and ammos from the US, Austria, and Israel among others and makes money off this importation via wholesale or retail. A very legit business with very legal profits.

This family business is an equal opportunity profiteer as long as one has the capacity to pay. The PNP and the NPA, legit security companies and suspicious private armies, your neighbor and your grannie. As long as you have the right amount of cash, you'll get your highly desired caliber. Literally, a bang for your buck. Or as @Pia would say, "for realz."

But no. Rafa just couldn't be bothered. He would rather

wear a fucking tie and leather shoes and slug it out 9 to fucking 5 for mere loose change. And for what? A fucking membership to the Social Security System? The government mandated thirteenth month pay? How much is a performance bonus worth compared to a grease money from a bulk sale to the PNP? Or a cut from the revolutionary tax levied by the NPA? It seems like Rafa is not only bad at Insta, my lurves, but he's also even worse at the math.

Now we come to the point in my story where I reveal the secret of all secrets of the biz.

Take note, my lurves, for this is the one secret that you should bookmark, share, heart, screenshot, and save.

And the secret is this: the only way to achieve success is to be born into success.

In other words: the only way to generate money is to be born into money.

And this is why all of us, except Rafa, are into the family business. Our family business.

Just what do we have to do to be in the family business?

It's so hard AF, my lurves. You wouldn't believe it, but we are expected to be desired and beautiful, avoid pissing off our fam, and enjoy the money that comes like clockwork into our trust fund.

So difficult.

Sometimes, I even think that life is just so unfair.

This is why I do my styling and shit, even taking, for the right amount of Benjamins, some gig that uses my awesomeness as an—fuck this word—influencer. And of course, that weekly performance art on my OnlyFans. With a little help from top-of-the-line snow, I just think of these side hustles as my therapy. For the alternative would be madness.

Anyhoo.

The family business. Right.

@Pia's fam purveys jologization.

Now my lurves, this makes a lot of sense as Pia's family is as jologs as they come. And as such, they are responsible for jologizing tho jologs like they have never been jologized before. What they term as all things media and entertainment. They are purveyors of all the stupidity on TV. Telenobelas, game shows, reality shows, cooking shows, comedy shows, variety shows, you name it, @Pia's fam has produced and aired it. Including movies they call films, shot and cut and screened or streamed in an assembly-line they call a studio using the same cast, the same crew, the same cliches. They say they also have a news and info arm but we all know the money comes from the jologs and not the self-proclaimed intellectuals of our land. They've also read the climate correctly and have gone into new media, manufacturing clickbait articles and passing it off as news on top of the legit ones they copy and paste from more reliable sources.

@Basti's fam is into land grabbing.

What they call real estate development. The shit that the gods no longer make no matter how many physicists explain that the universe is continuing to expand or that there will always be the next frontier. All bullshit, if @Basti's fam is to be believed. The earth is shrinking with every baby born alive, and soon, we will run out of space. According to them, the only futures that we all should be investing in are not crypto or wine or art but soil. Land. Earth. Real estate. And so, like modern-day Magellans they continue to map out and subjugate any and all square meter of land that is up for grabs like there is no tomorrow. To the point that they practically own the whole country. And don't get me started on their properties abroad, thinly disguised as a pied-à-terre in all seven continents, where the whole family, instead of traveling or vacationing, get to "summer" or "winter."

@Vicente's fam is into white-collar crime.

But everyone calls it banking and finance. Like highway robbery but high-end, committed in the well-lit and airconditioned rooms by well-dressed and well-mannered bankers under the command of the patriarch. The same business model accepted worldwide. You willingly give them your money and they willingly rob you of the money that your money produces. You call it savings and investments, they call it profits and fortunes. To be clear, this is different from the usurious loans and schemes which rob you not just of your money but your properties as well through the very legal ways of foreclosures and forfeitures in the event of a default. And what good would a banking family be without the occasional foray into laundering ill-gotten money, of which half the cash currently in circulation certainly belongs to? It's an icky job, but hey, this dirty money won't clean itself. Have you ever asked yourselves why a bank is as highly guarded as a maximum-security prison? Yes, the criminals in residence need to be secured.

And what of my fam, my lurves?

Well.

Ma famille is in the salvation business. The rest of the world calls it politics but whatevs. And we do this salvation from wholesale to retail, from the grand to the granular, from the national to the local. One could say that Gino is a puppeteer. From his perch in the hallowed halls of the Senate, Gino can make things happen and save souls down to the poorest barrios and the farthest of barangays via his bills and his programs. And also, through party alignment of the kapitans and the konsehals who know that they better obey his word to the letter. Including the punctuation of that letter. Otherwise, they get none of that precious pork or the occasional calamity fund and infra project. Gino is a Senator as was his father before him, as was his father, too, and well, you get the idea, my lurves. Others may argue that what we have is a political dynasty. I would argue right back that what we have is a family so devoted to saving this nation that everyone is making the sacrifice into making that salvation happen. "For god so loved the world..." if I recall John 3:16 right as what Sister Heidi has drilled into our brains.

Yes, my lurves, saving the world involves a lot of moolah.

And this Friday night, this moolah, my moolah, is being plundered by @Vicente, who is now Ferdinand.

Although it is still very early on this particular Friday, all I could do is wonder, when will he ever be done?

Chapter Twenty-Seven

I t turns out that the retard is not yet done, no sir.

After all, as my Lolo always says, the night is still young and so are we.

Vicente, or that Ferdinand, places on the white center table the money that he has liberated from my person. A pittance really compared to Mitzi's cash. He also divides my moolah into two.

And then he continues speaking.

"Now, a strong republic needs a strong citizenry. That's why we need to strengthen our rice production. We need an honest agricultural reform. We need to empower our farmers. We need a competitive rice research institute. We need a miracle rice that would feed not just the Filipino people but the rest of Asia, and even the world! With that in mind, I thank you for your contribution."

Just like before, he pockets half the money.

"This will go into my foreign investments. Gold bullions and treasury bonds hidden in a few Swiss banks. A couple of legit investments in New York for the sake of the almighty dollar. Asia's strongman needs an impervious financial strength. This presidential power, even when I finally become a dictator, might not last forever, unless I anoint myself King the soonest. King Ferdinand the First of the Maharlika Kingdom. Has a nice ring to it, wouldn't you agree? In the meantime, what better provision for power but untold wealth?"

Vicente, or that Ferdinand, then turns to Basti and does the same systematic robbery.

And yes, no other word could describe what is happening now but robbery. Of everything.

And by everything, I mean everything including Basti's emergency funds.

For a second, Basti looks at Vicente, at that Ferdinand, unmoving.

But for whatever reason, maybe he wants to be in the game too, or maybe he also was possessed, Basti starts to empty his pockets.

After, he proceeds to take out whatever funds he has secreted in his bedroom. Yes, from a military-grade safe the color of gunmetal gray, the only thing in his penthouse that is not white as fucking white. And the safe is ginormous, too.

Now, as I have said, Basti's family business is real estate. They buy lands from direct owners and foreclosed properties from the banks scattered all over the islands and then lease them out to developers. Some, especially in remote areas, they keep for themselves mostly as their own secret vacation hideaways.

It must have been a good year as Basti produced a lot of dough.

And by a lot, I mean a lot.

Most of what he produced from the bedroom are still in bricks bound with the *Bangko Sentral* seal, the kind of cash that could either come from the government treasury or a crime lord. Not that there is a difference between the two these days. I should know, we are in the peacekeeping hardware business, remember?

I was once brought with my father as he was making a sale to the head of the PNP Counter-Intelligence Group and the exchange happened in one of the warehouses in Camp Crame where piles upon piles of cold hard cash are stored. I shit you not. Bricks upon bricks of newly minted cash shrink-wrapped and cubed and stacked in pallets like the fucking canned goods aisle in S&R.

If seeing Mitzi loaded is enough to strengthen my resolve to quit my job by Monday morning, seeing Basti's cash makes me smack myself for not doing it this very Friday.

Really. I cannot wait to quit and get my ass into the family business. Our family business. *My* family business.

My first thought is: Holy Mother of Fuck, Basti! That, right there, is what you would call as a shitload of dough.

Now I know why he laughed that time when I showed Basti my SSS and TIN IDs as proof that I am a contributing member of our society the moment I got my first paycheck.

My succeeding thoughts are: are you dealing blue? Are you The Danger? Shall I call you Heisenberg?

For surely that kind of moolah could have only come from something illegal.

And finally: Holy Mother of Fuck! Are you really giving all that hard cash to that retard Vicente, or that Ferdinand, who, with every second that passes seems to be getting full possession of our friend?

As if reading my fucking mind, Vicente, or that Ferdinand, speaks again.

"Now, what would be a great republic without arts and culture? We need a film center! A cultural center! An international convention center! We need the boxing fight of the century to happen right in our country! Call it Thrilla in

Manila! We need the Miss Universe crowned in one of these beautiful islands! But why stop there? We need to import The Beatles to this side of the pacific!"

After he has looted the safe and has taken all of Basti's money, Vicente, or that Ferdinand, does something different. This time, he pockets all the cash and turns to Pia.

And of course, the fucker speaks. Again.

"Meldy, my dear Meldy. All these are for you, my love. You will no longer be shopping in Gaisano. Or even in Rustan's. Your new playground will now be Harrods, Bergdorf Goodman, Le Bon Marché. All the shoes, all the perfumes, all the lingerie in the world will be yours. Everything that you desire. Everything. My people follow me, you know that. And who do I follow? You! Of course, my dear Meldy, you! Only you!"

Fucking weird as fuck, even on a Friday, right? Even with us having a sip of Moët being chased by an even more expensive cocaine.

What's even weirder is that Pia, whom I had noticed earlier to be enjoying all the attention, now looks like she is getting wet from all that talk about shoes and perfumes and panties.

"Ohhheeemmmgeee!" Pia says. "For realz? You are not sucking my dick? I am literally getting all the feelz here."

That girl talk with Mitzi during her entrance into the penthouse comes back. That how's the weather question that Mitzi has volleyed to Pia.

With a very clear translation: I know you and Vicente are fucking each other's brains out behind Basti's back. You go gurrrlll! Get some action into that new-shaven pink!

But could it be true?

That Vicente, that retard, is actually fucking Pia? Pia! My one true love aside from Mitzi! My BAE who is getting away!

Suddenly, with this—what? doubt? context?—no, the word is epiphany, something I learned from Lolo the *Arsobispo*, I sense that Pia feels entitled to receive these promised shoes and whatever the fuck else from both Basti and Vicente.

Pia is an equal opportunity lover after all. She expects the same flattery and flirtation from her boyfriend and whoever else she is fucking on the side.

Mitzi whips out her iPhone again. With fingers fast as fuck, she snaps a couple of shots of the money on the table, whatever is still not pocketed by Vicente, or that Ferdinand.

She writes something, the keyboard sound effects in cadence with what she says out loud.

"Ferdinand Marcos," Mitzi says, "has...just...robbed...us, exclam. All...of...our...moolah...gone, exclam, exclam, exclam, devil emoji."

She copies and pastes and posts and works her way into her various social media accounts. Various sent chimes come, tweeting and swooshing inside Basti's crib.

Basti, somehow, is taken out of his fucking stupor. This, after handing his shit to Vicente, or that Ferdinand. He finally notices Pia's reaction to what has been promised her, shoes and perfumes and panties.

He then joins his hands with ours again as Vicente, or that Ferdinand, still unmindful, continues to pocket his loot, his newfound wealth, every fucking *centimo* that he doesn't have to work for.

"Hurry the fuck up, Basti," Mitzi says. "Stop sucking my balls and say that prayer again."

We all do the upside-down sign of the cross. Clasp each other's hands. Close our eyes tight. Hold our breaths.

Then Basti says the prayer again. In that dead speech that could have been Latin. That obscure language of the sacred or the street slang of the profane.

"GIGANTVM PENISIVM," I hear him whisper as he starts his prayer.

And this is precisely when this particular Friday night accelerates to a what-the-fuck level.

Chapter Twenty-Eight

What the fuck?

And no, I don't mean Rafa's pathetic amount of cash that was easily looted by @Vicente, who is now Ferdinand. Loose change really that isn't even worth robbing, IMHO.

I mean the words that @Vicente, who is now Ferdinand is mumbling to himself. And even weirder is that he's no longer speaking in the third.

He keeps repeating something about his internet presence. And having a legion of fans. Friends. Followers. His people and his public that's hungry for his feeds, his posts, his snaps, his vids. Something about content being key. How great content travels the world. How great content trends worldwide.

And get this, my lurves. These words make the hairs on my neck stand up and I get some major goosebumps. Now, you all know that I am fearless as fuck. Fierce as fuck. But these words somehow remind me of my family business. Yes, that salvation business everyone terms as politics.

@Vicente, who is now Ferdinand, continues.

How he is going to bankroll his brand. With my moolah. Fuck me, my lurves, but I have just become an angel investor, a *venture capitalist, a Peter fucking Thiel to @Vicente, who is now Ferdinand, like he is some fucking unicorn destined to make it big in the biz. He is even doing an Elon Musk, anointing himself King of his very own kingdom! Does that make @Pia his C? Will he sperminate her and make her his baby mama?*

But he's not yet done

Not in the fucking least.

After robbing Rafa blind, @Vicente, who is now Ferdinand, moves on to @Basti.

And here's another WTF part, my lurves.

@Basti obliges.

Like being robbed by @Vicente is the most normal thing on this stormy Friday night.

@Basti actually leads @Vicente, who is now Ferdinand, into his sanctvm sanctorvm where he keeps a safe the size of an upright freezer. I know this because this safe is the only thing in his penthouse that is not bone white. It's not an eyesore, per se, but it somehow looks out of place with the whole interior aesthetic since it's colored space gray like a MacBook Pro. And matte as one, too.

K. I see that I am wrong about that.

The safe being the only thing not white in the place.

For inside the biometric-protected safe are loads of cash that's also colored blue. No, not as blue as my Benjamins but blue as in the thousand-peso bills. Newly minted and mechanically wrapped and packed by one of the modern machines of our very own Central Bank.

And if my eyes are to be believed, there is so much cash that @Basti can buy a small African nation. Maybe Burundi, Rwanda, or Djibouti.

Now, I've always known that @Basti is loaded AF. Family business, remember? But I just cannot process that amount of newly minted dough sitting inside the safe, the same way I just cannot process why he is giving it all away. Something or other is going on. Surely, @Basti must be cooking up a plan?

And now @Vicente, who is now Ferdinand, with all the moolah in the world at his disposal, moves on to his brand goals. He is planning things that in his mind will stick, go viral, and trend as fuck. Staging events on the international scale. Sports events, music festivals, beauty pageants, the works. You know, like a real—fuck this word—influencer!

L'horreur!

Could it be?

It couldn't.

It just couldn't!

And get this, my lurves, the shit gets even weirder.

Because @Vicente, who is now Ferdinand, is back to calling @Pia, that adorable little slut, as his Meldy.

And again, who the fuck is Meldy?

The scoop here is that he is fessing up.

That all this robbery and thievery are being committed in her name. That she's the one who's going to reap the rewards of his efforts. He even name-dropped a couple of places in Europe that he will take her shopping as well as the boring crap usually found in a swag. Stilettoes and fragrances and lingerie, how fucking original. According to @Vicente, who is now Ferdinand, the world belongs to @Pia, who is now Meldy, because she is his one and only BAE.

How about that, my lurves.

Confiiirrrmmmed! That my sus earlier couldn't be any truer! These two are totes boning each other to death.

@Pia replies with a premature orgasm translated into human language. I could even tell by the way she shivers that she is squirting a little like she always does when I make her cum on my OnlyFans.

"Ohhheeemmmgeee! For realz? You are not sucking my dick? I am literally getting all the feelz here."

I, of course, have something to say about this madness.

And so, I tweeted again, in the hope that someone, anyone, would have an idea as to who this fucking Ferdinand is.

"Ferdinand Marcos has just robbed us! All of our moolah gone!!!" I add a devil emoji before I send it into the aether. And just to be safe, I send this message to the rest of my active socials.

@Basti hears @Pia's cum voice and he finally wakes up from his space travels and he joins us back on this Earth on this Friday.

He leads us in doing the inverted sign of the cross and once again joins our hands.

We all get the idea and I tell him to hurry the fuck up.

As @Basti starts saying his prayer, the fucking storm unleashes another attack.

Chapter Twenty-Nine

The fucking storm redoubles its attack. The thunder and the lightning are now joined by the wind that sounded like, to use the words of my Lolo, the weeping and gnashing of fucking teeth. The sound is maddening. Like a thousand widows howling to the heavens. Layered with a million skulls being drummed with bones.

And the power, with perfect timing, goes out too.

Everyone in the penthouse is either a shadow or a silhouette, a black and white diorama framed by the floor-to-ceiling glass window. All of us are frozen.

A flash of lightning comes, so bright and so powerful that it leaves a blinding retinal echo in my head I just couldn't shake off. A snapshot of us is imprinted in my mind, a negative that fails to develop as the meager light fails spectacularly to make it whole, like an image that does not resolve, a canvas that is not finished.

This is followed by a crack of thunder, tearing, to use another of my Lolo's words, the firmaments and the fundaments.

Heaven and earth are at war and hell is joining this Friday night party.

The power comes back on.

When my eyes adjust to the gloom, the room is now noticeably darker than before. I try to convince myself that this darkness is just due to the partial blindness from that fucking lightning show moments before.

But.

But...

But the room remains dark.

And it is at this point, if we think of our story as a novel, that we head into Act 2.

Chapter Thirty

And it is at this point in my story, if you think of this as all happening on my Insta, that I drop an unexpected post and pivot.

But first, the storm.

This fucking storm that is fucking up my brand aesthetic. This fucker is crashing this invite-only party and making a scene the way a photobomber ruins a well-art-directed shot.

Swear to gods, hope to die, this storm is alive. And unreasonable as fuck. It is throwing a teenage tantrum, messing with the power so that the whole penthouse, no, the whole city is plunged into total darkness.

And that noise!

The apartment is closer to the heavens than it is to the ground but I can hear hell opening up, working its way upwards. It could just be thunder but the whole place trembles every time it cracks. Every explosion is a knock on the fucking door like the storm wants to come in and have its share of the bubbly and the snow.

Not to be outdone, lightning comes with every thunder, torching the skies, lighting it up so that we can see the wind and the rain whatever the fuck it is that the storm is unleashing this very Friday My mo day.

And then blindness.

The power is suddenly back on that it hurts my eyes.

When my eyes adjust, I know that the room is darker than before. A gloom that has been shyly hiding in the corners and the crevices of the cavernous penthouse is now brave enough to creep out. It is all over the place. Like a fucking Insta vignette that is out of whack. Or a smudged camera lens that layers the frame with grime.

No matter how I squint my eyes, the whole place, despite the arc lamp and the ceiling lights being back on, remains a bit dark.

And here, my lurves, is the fucking drop.

@Vicente speaks again, this time back in the third.

Chapter Thirty-One

By the time the reverb of the thunder fades out, the first thing I hear is Vicente.

"Vicente is confused. Vicente wants to know what the fuck is up," Vicente says.

Thank fuck, the retard is back.

"Vicente?" Pia says. "For realz, is that you? Answer me!"

Vicente repeats his questions, still in the third person, and that seems to settle everyone.

Well, except for Basti who is quiet. Unmoving. As if looking at everything that is happening inside his crib from afar.

And then he speaks.

And this is when we know that whoever the fuck possessed Vicente, is now taking a stranglehold of Basti.

Chapter Thirty-Two

(A)Basti is being possessed. And the very same worm that has infiltrated @Vicente is now initiating a reprog of his operating system, a rewire of his control center.

The leet is hacked.

The leet is fucked.

The leet that is @Basti is now Ferdinand.

And how do I know this, my lurves?

Because @Vicente, the lousy little retard, is back with us, speaking in the third.

"Vicente is confused. Vicente wants to know what is happening."

See?

He has landed in the land of the living.

@Pia is a bit sus, which, of course, is understandable.

"Vicente? For realz, is that you? Answer me!"

I could even smell a hint of disappointment in her quesh.

@Vicente answers @Pia and it is also his talking in the third that reassures her, that adorable little slut.

I breathe a sigh of relief.

And then @Basti, who is now Ferdinand, speaks.

Some crap about life being a struggle.

Chapter Thirty-Three

" If we accept life as a struggle, and history as the continuing struggle for freedom, we realize the necessity of a revolution, and from that, the imperative of a militant creed. I believe, therefore, in the necessity of Revolution as an instrument of individual and social change, and that its end is the advancement of human freedom. I believe that the only reactionary resistance to radical change will make a Jacobin, or armed, revolution, inevitable but that in a democratic society, revolution is of necessity, constitutional, peaceful, and legal. I believe that while we have utilized the Presidential powers to dismantle the bloody revolution and its rightist, communists, and other apparatus, we must not fail our people; we must replace the bloody revolution with the authentic revolution—liberal, constitutional, and peaceful."

Basti, or that Ferdinand, continues but my mind stops processing the words at "bloody revolution."

This is getting weird.

This is getting beyond weird.

This is getting beyond *beyond*.

Meanwhile, the speech, if that is indeed a speech and not

another incantation or prayer or what the fuck ever, continues.

"I believe that our realization of the common peril, our complete understanding of our national condition, will unite us in our democratic institutions and offer, finally, our citizens the opportunity of making the most and the best of themselves. I believe that democracy is the revolution, that it is today's revolution. This is my fighting faith."

Upon hearing these words, I accept that indeed, it is not Basti speaking. While he is intelligent in his own way and could make up some interesting game on a boring Friday night, Basti could neither compose nor memorize that kind of speech even if his life depended on it.

Fighting faith, my ass.

Mitzi's phone starts having an epileptic attack again. The pings and the alerts, the replies and the shares give her iPhone a kind of seizure so disturbing that it threatens to jump off the center table.

"Is there an update on our little situation here?" I ask.

Mitzi fingers her device, alternating between a million social media apps before she replies.

"Thirty-seven point nine million hearts and thirty-two million point seven retweets. But not one fucking woke knows who this Ferdinand is," Mitzi says. "And oh, lots of 'LOLs' and 'awesomes.' That this fucker is robbing us blind is kind of funny, I guess."

Now, please allow me to break the narrative for a moment so we can unpack this. Think of our story as a novel and this is one of those annoying asterisks that you have to read at the bottom of a page.

Here goes: we are in the age of Google, Edward fucking Snowden, and facial recognition software.

And yet, no one knows who this Ferdinand is.

Chew on that for a second.

To continue.

Vicente, newly freed from the possession of that Ferdinand, speaks again.

"Vicente thinks that this is not funny. At all. If Basti was the one who did The Summoning and then he was the one that is possessed, well, fuck Vicente but it is highly suspect," Vicente says to all of us. "Isn't it?"

Everyone, except Basti of course, joins in to remind Vicente that the possession happened to him first.

Which, we all agree, is some kind of proof that the possession is indeed real.

For isn't whoever is possessed not supposed to be aware that he is possessed?

Mitzi reminds Vicente how he fleeced everyone.

Pia tears him a new one about calling her Meldy, emphasizing his promises of jewelry and perfume and lingerie, and shopping in London and New York and Paris, though I think that this is more of a reminder than a reproach.

My turn comes.

I tell Vicente how he slapped me like some *telenobela* character and how that almost wasted good Champagne.

Vicente, as could be expected, pleads not guilty to all of these, to use one of Lola's words, shenanigans, and so we continue with our assault.

"Ohhheeemgeee! My head literally exploded when you called me Meldy! I got all the feelz. For realz!" says Pia, who, despite not being made to part with her own hard-earned money, seems to be the most aggrieved party.

Ha! Hard-earned! I used that term, ironically, right?

As we are all giving Vicente a piece of our minds, Basti, or that Ferdinand who is now in full possession of his person, speaks.

"Fellow Filipinos. Now is not the time for all these petty concerns. We have much to do for this country and we cannot achieve it unless we are all united. Nefarious individuals are already grouping themselves. Plotting acts of rebellion against my government. It is paramount for the survival of our democracy that you all unite behind me and continue to follow my lead."

And so, Vicente hears for the very first time that very same Ferdinand who had earlier possessed his person order us around like a motherfucker the way he previously did.

Of course, this does not sit well with Vicente, he who has the—to use another of my Lola's words—temerity, to fuck Basti's girlfriend behind his back.

"Vicente finds this lame," Vicente says. "Lame as an old man's shriveled dick. Ha! Follow you? Vicente says that you need to stop this tomfoolery this very moment! Cease this faggotry at once!"

And what does he get from Basti, or that Ferdinand, for an answer?

A first-person singular punch in the face of course!

Beautiful!

And a real strong punch at that as Basti, unlike Vicente when he struck me, is not holding a drink this time.

Quick as a bullet, Basti's right hand hits Vicente, solid as fuck, his closed hand connecting with Vicente's fleshy cheek that comes with an ear-splitting sound. Fuck yes, that punchable face gets a proper punching with the holy righteous anger of the god of the Old Testament.

So beautiful!

"This administration will not tolerate dissent and insurrection, boy!" Basti, or that Ferdinand, says. "Have you no respect for your President?"

Vicente strikes back. Or, at least attempts to.

I say attempts to because Basti, or that Ferdinand, hits him again. The Biblical punch from earlier gets an upgrade to a Hollywood hit. It's now a one-way Fight Club as Basti, or that Ferdinand, unleashes an uppercut square under Vicente's left jaw.

Vicente loses his footing.

He staggers backwards.

Scrambles for purchase.

Catches Pia's arm.

And together, they fall down on the sofa.

Now that I know their backstory, I notice something in the way that they are holding each other, the way they are holding on to each other.

A familiarity.

As if they have been doing this for a long time.

The way they sat earlier with Pia's hand resting on Vicente's knee before it ever so slowly crawled up his inner thigh suddenly makes sense.

Vicente and not Basti, is Pia's BAE.

I take a look at Basti.

He seems oblivious to all this.

Like he is seeing Vicente only as a threat to his "Presidency" and someone who must stay down and be silenced. Not a rival to his girlfriend's heart.

"I am not allowing anyone to undermine the stability of this government," Basti, or that Ferdinand, says. "Is everybody clear on that?"

Chapter Thirty-Four

One thing is very clear to me, my lurves.

@Basti, who is now Ferdinand, is using some big words to articulate his brand purpose. It's like he is filling up a ginormous vision board not with visuals but with words. All the crap that he is saying won't even fit in a single tweet. Or even two. I get the fact that one of his action points is to replace the fakery of social media revolution with a real one. And that he must not fail his fans and his followers.

But don't we all?

Want a revolution, I mean?

And not fail our people and our public as we do it?

@Basti, who is now Ferdinand, might be using some big words that might just become so lit in a few it will totes magotes skip being street slang, or a t-shirt slogan, and head straight to corporate jargon.

But he's not entirely original, is he?

Revolution, my derrière.

I stand corrected, my lurves.

"Authentic revolution."

These are the words.

This is the brand goal.

I know. I know.

It's a bit sticky and some noob might tag this shit and it just might trend.

#AuthRev has a nice ring to it, to be honest.

And speaking of sticky shit and hashtaggable words, @Basti, who is now Ferdinand, continues mumbling about giving his fans opportunities and his followers empowerment, and that by democratizing shit, he can make his revolution happen.

And a lot of other big words that still won't fit in a hundred and forty characters.

But here's another diamond from @Basti, who is now Ferdinand.

"Fighting faith."

Yep. #FightingFaith is trendable AF.

Swear to gods, hope to die, these words are getting weird as fuck.

Not the faith but the fighting part.

Because a fight indeed erupts on this stormy Friday night.

My iPhone starts screaming for attention once again. Notifications are pouring in and I pick it up and toggle between my socials, combing through all the replies that are still streaming in as I am reading them.

As I have expected, not one of you fuckers know who this Ferdinand is.

Not a single one of you who number in the millions know. And not even an anonymous rando lurking on my posts can enlighten me.

I am so wet at the thought that I would be doxing this Ferdinand like he has never been doxed before but all of you motherfuckers are clamblockers. What I get is a lot of LOLs and awesomes. And more requests for pussy pics and squirt vids. As if I give these for free.

Now, my lurves, think of this as a point in my story where I use one of those fab question stickers. Using my personalized font that follows my brand aesthetic, of course.

And the quesh is this: why is it that in this age of TikTok and Twitter, Facebook and YouTube, WhatsApp and Viber, Twitch and Insta, PornHub and OnlyFans, this Ferdinand is a ghost?

I don't know him.

You don't know him.

Nobody knows him.

Why the fuck is that?

Anyhoo.

@Vicente, now freed from that Ferdinand, once again speaks in the third.

Turns out that he has done some mental jujitsu and has his very own sus about @Basti. How, according to @Vicente, @Basti is just faking it, his being possessed and all since he was the one who uttered the fucking prayer for The Summoning.

Confiiirrrmmmed!

That @Vicente was indeed possessed by that Ferdinand. And also how he is now freed from his grasp.

Everyone gives @Vicente a throwback.

Moi? I recount how he Hoovered my moolah. My hard-earned moolah. My Benjamins.

Rafa relates about the bitchslap that he suffered and the precious bubbly that was wasted.

@Pia reminds him what he has promised her. The travels, the threads, eau de toilette, and the rest of the crap that he has sworn to do. And of course, him calling her "Meldy." And how her head "literally exploded." And how she got "all the feelz" and all "for realz." What an adorable little slut.

And then @Basti, who is now Ferdinand, speaks again.

Get this, my lurves.
     He wants to do a collab.
     A sort of cross-branding.
     And as if it is not funny enough, @Basti, who is now Ferdinand, gives a reason. That other brands are appropriating his awesomeness, coopting his brand, grabbing a piece of the pie of his market share, pilfering precious eyeballs, messing up with his metrics, and eating up his moolah.
     Thing is, I never do collabs. Ever.
     Especially now when @Basti, who is now Ferdinand, clarifies that his idea of a collab is that I should friend him, fan him, follow him.
     Jamais!
     So.
     Not a collab, but an order then.
     Well.
     This also sounds weird as fuck to @Vicente, who, let us not forget was the one ordering us around to call him as our "leader" mere minutes ago. And that bitchslap he has gifted Rafa! Also, the thievery of my Benjamins!
     And so, he does what only @Vicente could do.
     Impugn @Basti's masculinity in the third.
     "Vicente finds this lame. Lame as an old man's shriveled dick. Ha! Follow you? Vicente says that you need to stop this tomfoolery this moment! Cease this faggotry at once!"
     And this is how, on this stormy Friday night, I find myself in the middle of a fight.
     @Basti, who is now Ferdinand, punches @Vicente. In the face like a proper gentleman.
     The closed fist connects and sends @Vicente backwards but he does not fall down. At least not yet.

@Basti, who is now Ferdinand, shouts something about not taking any shit from anyone. Also, something about respect.

Credit where credit is due, but @Vicente, unlike Rafa with that royal bitchslap, at least makes an attempt to fight back.

Except that @Basti, who is now Ferdinand, releases another cracker of a punch that catches @Vicente square under his chin.

Like one of those 500 fps photo-sonic shots that is best for cum vids, @Vicente loses his footing, and slowly collapses, wildly flailing his arms.

The slow-mo continues as he somehow manages to hold on to @Pia.

And like the couple that they are, they hold on to each other for their lives as they both surrender to gravity.

Confiiirrrmmmed AF!

@Vicente and @Pia are in each other's arms, on the sofa. As per yoozh, she is on top. She has always preferred to be on top as it seems to be the only way she can get off. Just look for the latest ep of our girl-to-girl ep on Only Fans and you'll see what I mean. And if you're not a patron, remember that the code FRIDAY15! expires at midnight.

Anyhoo.

While they are dry-humping each other like high schoolers in the back pew of the school chapel, I take a look at @Pia.

That adorable little slut.

The thunder and the lightning, the wind and the storm, and all the weird shit is no match for the purity of my rage that's going nuclear inside my awesomeness.

Now I have to fess up, my lurves.

I decide right then to violate the sanctity of the Girl Code.

Chapter Thirty-Five

Let me just say that there is such a thing as a Bro Code. You know what I mean. Bros before hoes.

I also know that there is such a thing as a Girl Code, too. An example would be: fries before guys.

Bro Code, Girl Code. Same difference. Different sameness. We all look out for each other. We are our brother's keeper, as Lolo used to say. Like what Cain was to Abel. Ooops, wrong example. My bad.

This stormy Friday night, Mitzi throws the Girl Code out the floor-to-ceiling window with the following words, words that give each and every one of us a collective in-breath.

"Undermine what government, you dumb fuck?" Mitzi says. "Don't you see that your girlfriend is fucking someone else? And just in case it is not so obvious, Ferdinand, Sir, that other dude is Vicente."

Pia shoots Mitzi a look that could only be described as savage. Or brutal. Or killer.

Nothing could convey pure hostility and distilled antagonism more than Pia's eyes, something that makes me wonder whether their friendship is just a disguise waiting to be uncovered, a mask begging to be ripped off.

Superficial. Pretense. Artifice. Maybe my one and true loves, my BAEs, hated each other AF all along? Maybe they are not frenemies but enemies for real? Or as Pia would say, for realz?

But.

But...

But!

Here's the thing.

Basti, or that Ferdinand, is not in the least affected by what Mitzi has just said and even by the way Pia reacted to her words.

More important things are on his mind.

"That is a blatant violation of a direct order from the Commander-in-Chief of this great Republic," Basti, or that Ferdinand, says. "Before things get any worse, now would be the time to curtail rebellion and destabilization. I am hereby enacting Presidential Decree Number 33 to penalize the printing and possession of leaflets and other materials and even graffiti that undermine the integrity of the government. No one, and I say no one, will have the right to speak a single seditious word. Everything shall be cleared by both the Department of Public Information and the Office of the Press Secretary, from TV to the radio to the newspapers to the wire agencies, and that includes all utterances."

Now, all that crap about the Presidential Decree number something or other is more mind-boggling than Basti's fucked up prayer in Latin.

What does that even mean? No, not the GIGANTVM PENISIVM but the right to say seditious words!

And also: leaflets, newspapers, wire agencies? What the actual fuck are these?

And clearing shit with the Public Information Office? This, when everyone can say brilliant stuff on Twitter and Facebook and Twitch and TikTok that border on poetry and he wants us to do what?

So, of course, not one of us gives a fuck.

Meanwhile, Vicente, to defend himself, starts to verbally attack Mitzi.

In all the glory of the third person singular as only that retard can pull off.

"Vicente thinks that wasn't cool, Mitzi. Malicious, is what that was. To think that Vicente believes you and Pia are the best of friends. That you and Vicente are cool. Why do you have to do that? Are your creative endeavors stuck in a fucking rut, you fucking free spirit? Vicente thinks that your art pretentions and artist affectations have got to fucking stop before you do some serious damage to real artists who have real talent and not just Daddy's money. Fashion styling? Modeling? Vlogging? Please. You're just a slut with a laptop. A cheap ho with an iPhone. Do the world a fucking favor and just stop with your fucking influencing. Although Vicente guesses that it is not your so-called career or whatever the fuck it is you're doing for the moment as you wait for your life to end the suffering that's driving you fucking insane. Vicente thinks that you are not getting any. Seriously. Is that shaved vagina of yours drying up from lack of action? You gotta get some, Mitzi! And I don't mean you doing yourself for some crappy vids on your OnlyFans!"

Ouch!

Double ouch!

Before I could say a single word to Mitzi's defense, Vicente, that retard, attacks me, too.

"Well. Vicente thinks that there's Rafa. You would still do Mitzi, wouldn't you, Rafa? And hell, looking at you now, Vicente can tell that you still wanna do her. Fuck, Rafa! You might still even love her! Vicente thinks that you two would make quite the fucking couple. Haha! Fucking couple, get it? The loser pretending to be an artist and another loser pretending to be a corporate whore who couldn't even afford a bottle of beer on a Friday night. Isn't that the reason why you, Rafa, are always sucking up to either Vicente or Basti, hell even Pia, and yes, even Mitzi, for the fucking free beer? Vicente knows that you are our charity case. You wanna run to Daddy, don't you, Rafa? Wanna grab some of the easy money from Daddy's little gunrunning business? Have you resigned yet from being a corporate monkey like some fucking peon? Oh, fuck yes, Rafa, Vicente knows all these."

Ouch!
      Ouch!
      Triple ouch!
      Now that actually hurts more than the fucking slap.
      It really does.
      Only because I know that Vicente is no longer under the influence of that Ferdinand. And that means that he is saying these things out of his own mind.
      That retard really called me a charity case!
      Is that what he thinks of me?
      Me?!
      The only one in this fucking room on this fucking Friday night who could actually be a fucking woke!
      And I am sure as fuck that I am the only one among us who has a fucking Social Security Number, a valid Tax ID number, and an active Pag-Ibig membership.
      The only one with a *quincenas* paycheck and a yearly thirteenth month pay. With at least two—two!—annual

performance bonuses! The only one with a platinum AmEx that is not an extension card from Daddy's account. The only one with a fucking Range Rover—the preferred vehicle of choice of us successful gunrunners because appearances have to be maintained in the biz—that is not a gift from Mommy.

Does this fucking retard even have an iota of the idea of what he is talking about?

No! Of course not. He is clueless AF.

What does he know about a nine-to-five job when all his life, he has been collecting an allowance from his daddy?

Who, of all things, happens to be a fucking banker.

You all have heard the saying, right?

Give a man a gun and he robs a bank. Give the man a bank and he robs the world.

That's what Vicente's daddy is, a fucking career criminal. The only difference between him and the members of The Quiapo Joggers' Society is a suit and a tie. But at least those fucking snatchers in Quiapo have authenticity on their side. They are fucking hungry. Which makes them fucking hardcore.

And Vicente? His Daddy?

They are fucking profiteers from this banking crime! Parasites!

Now, who is Vicente to, and again I am using my Lola's words, impugn my masculinity with this kind of unfounded, vindictive rumor?

I am not about to let that shit pass.

This is fucking war.

And I am going Old Testament on his retarded ass.

Chapter Thirty-Six

How very Old Testament.
            My holy righteous anger targeting @Basti, who is now Ferdinand.
      And @Vicente.
And @Pia.

I dox @Pia like that adorable little slut has never been doxed before. Looking straight into the beautiful eyes of @Basti, who is now Ferdinand, I unpack my truth. That his BAE is totally fucking another dude who is not some rando ordered from the internet, but none other than his BFF @Vicente.

@Vicente who speaks in the third is none other than @Pia's second.

And let's not forget that @Basti is not even her first.

I even pointed an accusatory finger at both @Pia and @Vicente, at these two fuckers who are still in each other's arms despite having gotten up after they fell on the sofa earlier.

I know. I know.

It so fucking hurts, my lurves.

To see the hurt that I am causing @Pia.

I Only Hurt the Ones I Love. *I remember one of my most-hearted posts on Insta. It was true when I dropped it last February the thirteenth, and it is still true this very Friday.*

In her eyes, I see the pure love that @Pia has for me as only one BFF can have for another. She is murdering me with her looks and doing an autopsy with her mind and hosting a dope funeral party with her soul. I am already dead to her and not even my awesomeness can resurrect me.

But how will I ever know that I really love her if I don't hurt @Pia? Right, my lurves?

And also: how will @Pia ever know that I really love her if I don't hurt her?

The only comfort that I can think of to soothe my breaking heart is that @Pia would not hesitate to do what I have done if the situation were reversed. I know that she, too, has only pure love for me. Besties forevs, that's what we are.

And then @Basti, who is now Ferdinand, speaks.

Turns out that what I just did is a fucking no-no. And that the kind of disruption that I just architected is not to be tolerated. As if I am one of those disgusting trolls wrecking social media. The bashers. The haters. And what does @Basti, who is now Ferdinand, want to do? To make himself the one and the only moderator of all things being said. Not a single word is to be uttered without his greenlight. Not a single post is to be uploaded without his thumbs up. Not a single feed is to be updated without his all-clear.

Yep, my lurves. I am getting moderated like fuck. Across all social media platforms.

L'horreur!

This is tyranny in the 360.

As puzzling as his fucked up prayer that is ABSVRDVM PASSWORDVM.

I give zero fucks to this nonsense, obvs. Because, Insta. And also, my awesomeness. Plus, who the fuck is he telling me to STFU?

And then @Vicente pipes in, and as per yoozh, the lousy little retard is speaking in the third.

And get this, my lurves. @Vicente got the first part of his message right. That he totes believes that @Pia and moi are besties forevs. Truth.

After that, he submarined his message to the lowest of the depths that he could possibly go.

@Vicente actually questions my creativity.

He tells me that I am nothing but a noob with an iPhone. I know. I know.

It really fucking hurts.

He calls me a fashion stylist! A vlogger! A model!

And, swear to gods, hope to die, he calls me a fucking—fuck this word—influencer!

But for the coup de grâce: he tells me that I am not getting any.

Yep, my lurves, there is no finessing it. @Vicente tells me to my face that I need to get laid. And not on OnlyFans but IRL.

Now that really hurts as fuck.

No, not this stupid thing about me not getting some, but the fact that he slammed and smeared and slurred my being a free spirit on OnlyFans.

I honestly expected something solid and sticky from @Vicente, he who speaks in the third and is an early adopter as any early adopter could be. He who reviews all things tech from the analog to the digital, from the vintage to the emerging, from the commercial to the illegal.

That @Vicente who speaks in the third but is first on all things tech.

That he would truly get what OnlyFans is all about. Yep,

above and beyond the curated porn sold at a premium to paying pervs.

Here's the thing, my lurves, the one thing that @Vicente fails to understand.

OnlyFans is the logical progression of social media.

It is an idea perfected.

It is an ideal achieved.

It is an ideality manifested.

I know. I know.

I have to unpack that, my lurves.

There is poverty porn, middle class porn, wealth porn, excess porn, property porn, apartment porn, hotel porn, resort porn, farm porn, city porn, architecture porn, small house porn, McMansion porn, village porn, condo porn, furniture porn, interior design porn, kitchen porn, living room porn, bedroom porn, décor porn, minimalist porn, brutalist porn, antiquities porn, art porn, modern art porn, the masters porn, street art porn, vintage porn, haute couture porn, street wear porn, sneakers porn, stiletto porn, jewelry porn, fragrance porn, watch porn, time piece porn, gadget porn, car porn, bike porn, motorbike porn, leather porn, pleather porn, lifestyle porn, travel porn, leisure porn, vacation porn, passport porn, mileage porn, first class porn, first class lounge porn, restaurant porn, speakeasy porn, bar porn, pub porn, pop up porn, dinner club porn, food truck porn, pool porn, jacuzzi porn, surf porn, skate porn, beach porn, mountain porn, plane porn, train porn, yacht porn, cruise porn, stocks porn, futures porn, investments porn, acquisitions porn, securities porn, profession porn, nerd porn, jock porn, alternative porn, hipster porn, party porn, social porn, solitude porn, poetry porn, prose porn, literary porn, transgressive porn, speculative porn, book porn, newspaper porn, magazine porn, zine porn, intellectual porn, pseudo-intellectual porn, anti-intellectual porn, awards porn, winner porn, loser porn, participation porn, trophy porn, medal porn, certificate porn, collectible porn, limited edition porn, action figure porn, doll porn, robot porn, film porn, photography porn, animation porn, TV porn, cinema porn, theater porn, streaming porn, music porn, pop porn, bubblegum pop porn, hip hop porn, glam porn, goth porn, heavy metal porn, exercise porn, spin porn, yoga porn, pilates porn, boxing porn, crossfit porn, dance porn, ballroom dancing porn, golf porn, running porn, walking porn, planting porn, plant porn, monstera porn, flower porn, crossbreed porn, food porn, fruit porn, vegetable porn, wine porn, scotch porn, small batch porn, craft beer porn, cigar porn, coffee porn, cold brew porn, kombucha porn, kimchi porn, bone broth porn, avocado porn, quacamole porn, cannabis porn, edibles porn, meat porn, steak porn, steak frites porn, fish porn, octopus porn, sushi porn, sashimi porn, pescatarian porn, vegetarian porn, vegan porn, freegan porn, scavenger porn, garbage porn, salvage porn, repurpose porn, remade porn, repair porn, restoration porn, renovation porn, charity porn, Samaritan porn, salvation porn, do-gooder porn, donation porn, donor porn, predator porn, victim porn, prosecution porn, defense porn, justice porn, injustice porn, jail porn, miscarriage of justice porn, gun porn, knife porn, sword porn, wedding porn, bride porn, bridesmaid porn, groom porn, groomsmen porn, husband porn, wife porn, couples porn, mistress porn, family porn, broken family porn, modern family porn, pregnancy porn, miscarriage porn, abortion porn, adoption porn, birthing porn, birthday porn, anniversary porn, middle age porn, sexagenarian porn, sickness porn, hospice porn, death porn.

There are all kinds of porn.

All delicious, all divine.

But what I do on my OnlyFans is porn porn.

Real porn.

And when I say real, I mean real

Because here's the thing, lurves.

When you are watching me do me on my OnlyFans, you don't just wish to watch. You yearn to do. You ache to be. How real is that?

That's real porn in real life.

Waxed, wet, welcoming.

And, très important, *cumming.*

With no fig leaf to cover my awesomeness the way that it was in the garden of fucking Edon.

Ask Sister Heidi if you don't believe me.

Self-trafficking is self-authorship is self-actualization.

But who am I kidding?

Unlike you, my lurves, that lousy little retard @Vicente will never get it.

Well.

I am at the very least, willing to try.

Except that before I could educate @Vicente with my truth, he assaults Rafa, who, I see, is about to say something.

Poor Rafa!

And again, @Vicente gets the first part of his verbiage right.

That Rafa still has the hots for me and would totes magotes fuck me if I give him the barest of a hint. This is truth.

But @Vicente just couldn't help himself. He dives into his own sinkhole and declares that we are meant for each other.

Then he gets even lower: he talks about Rafa's moolah. Or his lack of.

I know. I know.

That kind of talk is a sport among us, the moneyed, but it is just bad manners to talk about someone's lack of moolah when that someone is present. That's like resting your elbows on the dinner table. Or spitting cum instead of swallowing. That's just not done.

But @Vicente cannot be confined by the oppressive rules of polite society.

He continues his assault on Rafa, telling him to his face that he is a charity case. That Rafa is just Anna Delveying his way through life. That he can't even afford his own beer. That he is just grifting his existence, committing grand larceny by smoothly smooching my hard-earned moolah off moi since his corporate job will never amount to much as a revenue stream, especially if benchmarked against all my earnings from all my socials.

He even mocks Rafa about his family biz.

Yep, my lurves, the gunrunning thing.

The very lucrative salvation business.

And this is when Rafa hauls his ass off the sofa, plants his two feet in front of @Vicente, and stares at him in the eyes.

Chapter Thirty-Seven

And so I get up from the sofa and stare at Vicente. That retard. That fucking bearer of false witness. Those, right there, are my Lolo's words. The former *Arsobispo de Manila*, remember?

Yes, that's what Vicente is. A bearer of false witness.

And I am about to go Moses on his lying, slandering ass.

Then Basti, or that Ferdinand, speaks again.

"Listen! All of you! To curtail rebellion and destabilization, I hereby declare Presidential Decree Number 90, penalizing rumor mongering. And what is a rumor? A rumor, as defined by me, your President, is false news and fake information. Gossip and hearsay. Any unfounded speech, written or orally transmitted, and all forms of its repetitions and iterations that undermine the stability of this government. Any violators will be taken to military camps for detention and investigation."

I ignore Basti, or that Ferdinand.

Presidential Decree, my ass.

But.

But...

But!

Speaking of rumors, gossip, and hearsay, here's something juicy I keep hearing lately. And this I say to Vicente because I can play that game too.

"You may think you know shit about me. You may think of it as truth. But here is one true thing I know about you. Your family business is done. It is over, my friend. Your fucking money making machine has been devoured by the biggest bank on this side of the world, and you, Vicente, are living on borrowed time. Also borrowed land as all your properties has been ravaged by *Familia* Montes. See that treasure that you plundered earlier? Why do you think Basti is loaded as fuck? Because he is making a killing off all your properties! Your precious fucking real estate! Or should that be unreal estate? Surreal estate? So, retard, who is getting fucked in the ass by whom? Any moment now, you will be begging for your allowance from Basti. That's right, you'll be groveling like a dog looking for some discards. Let's see how that goes. Do you really think that Basti gives a fucking fuck about you? You think he cares about Pia? Pia! His girlfriend, who, so far has only gotten a fist bump tonight while he greeted Mitzti by swapping saliva with her. Better hold on to that moolah that you stole from us earlier, Vicente. Because those are our offerings, our contributions, our alms for we are all gathered her tonight for your wake. It's your funeral Vicente, and may you rest in fucking peace. Yes, you can't even afford your own send off to the great unknown. And yes, Vicente, you are already dead, you just don't know it yet."

Vicente, fast as the fucking lightning making a lightshow out the window, lets go of Pia and charges towards me.

It is at this point that Basti, or that Ferdinand, gives him a perfectly executed clothesline followed by an arm twist and a shoulder pin. It all happens very quickly. A WWF technic quickly mutating into a UFC tactic.

Vicente moves his lips, maybe to speak, maybe to howl in pain but Basti, or that Ferdinand, still doing his reptile embrace, grips the retard's mouth and shuts him the fuck up.

"No more acts of insurrection!" Basti, or that Ferdinand, says. "No more acts of violence! I hereby declare Presidential Decree 885 forbidding the creation of subversive organizations, the preparing of documents, leaflets, and any other types of publications, and advising and counseling members of subversive organizations. All these are punishable acts. This Republic must be safeguarded against communism!"

Vicente makes another attempt. Of fucking course, he does.

But all he could do is emit a muffled cry like a dog being muzzled as Basti, or that Ferdinand, squeezes the retard's mouth—and this time including his nose as an expert stranglehold—even harder.

Not even half a word of an insult escapes Vicente's lips.

Instead, what I hear is Basti, or that Ferdinand, praising himself for his stellar effort in subduing something subversive and detrimental to his great vision for our great republic.

It actually sounds ridiculous. Basti, or that Ferdinand, patting himself on the back for a job well done in restoring peace and order, all the while unseeing the reality and being out of touch with the unrest brewing in his very own crib.

This fucking Friday night, murder is no longer just confined to a look between two very beautiful girls hating each other to death.

Murder is about to get fucking real.

Chapter Thirty-Eight

M urder, like porn, is real as fuck.
       Trust me on this, my lurves.
       It is as real as this story that I am telling you.

Like moi, before Rafa can even unpack his mind and respond to the assault done by @Vicente, @Basti, who is now Ferdinand, speaks again.

And what does he say, my lurves?

Only that I am getting canceled.

If I continue posting and updating and uploading what is happening this very Friday night. And again, across all socials. He's really telling me to shut the fuck up.

Moi? Getting canceled? L'horreur!

And then Rafa, who has been silent since that time when he reminded me about friending him on Insta, finally speaks.

Credit where credit is due, but Rafa fucking nails it big time as he drops something radioactive.

Yes, my lurves, something so incendiary directed at none other than @Vicente.

Rafa goes full nuclear on @Vicente's slimy retarded ass.

And the bomb that he unleashes is this: @Vicente is broke AF.

If that is not fucking explosive, I don't know what the fuck is.

It turns out that @Vicente's criminal organization that is their family business they call banking and finance has been devoured by an even bigger criminal org. And not only that, all their properties in these beautiful islands have also been gobbled up by none other than, get ready, my lurves, @Basti's family.

Deleeesssh.

But wait, there's more.

It turns out that Rafa is also good at this insult thing. He trolls @Vicente with such artistry that for a moment I wonder if he deserves to be on Twitter.

Rafa offers all the moolah that @Vicente has forcibly taken earlier as his alms for @Vicente's funeral party.

Word.

So deleeesssh.

Rafa's reveal hits the target accurately like an intelligent missile that @Vicente lets go of @Pia and attempts to bitchslap him again.

Attempts.

For @Basti, who is now Ferdinand, fucks @Vicente up before he can even take a half step in the general direction of Rafa.

It's like a fucking threesome by an awesome throuple and I lurve it.

Homo erotica at its best with @Basti, who is now Ferdinand, pinning @Vicente down as Rafa stands immobile, maybe doing the math as to whom he should sodomize first and skewer in the mouth second. Decisions, decisions.

@Basti, who is now Ferdinand, speaks again.

According to him, trolling is now canceled AF.

Yes, my lurves, all of us inside the penthouse must shut the fuck up like we have never shut the fuck up before.

Otherwise, punishment.

I know. I know.

I seem to be heading into BDSM territory here.

Now you all know me, my lurves.

I am at least willing to try anything once. Anything. K, maybe even twice. Plus, I have nothing against a little spanking on this stormy Friday night. The last time I got spanked was for a vid on my OnlyFans. And again, a friendly reminder, the code expires soon. FRIDAY15! Don't forget the exclam.

Anyhoo.

Before I could get any spanking going, @Vicente, who is still pinned to the floor by @Basti, who is now Ferdinand, attempts to speak.

Attempts.

He never gets his third-person insanity out of his mouth as @Basti, who is now Ferdinand, shuts his cock holster for him.

For a second, for an eternity, everything is still and quiet.

Chapter Thirty-Nine

E verything is still and quiet.
       That is, until Vicente uncoils like a wound-up mousetrap and launches an assault. Towards me.

Another lightning move by Basti, or that Ferdinand, and the retard is pinned to the floor again.

So beautiful.

This time, Basti, or that Ferdinand, gets Vicente in a half-Nelson. From WWF to UFC, we are back in the classical Greco-Roman wrestling. It is kind of homoerotic, watching these two dudes locked in a grapple, stuck in a grip. With Basti's crotch right on top of Vicente's ass.

So beautiful to behold.

And so, of course, Basti, or that Ferdinand, unleashes a fucking speech again after releasing Vicente who has submitted and remains motionless.

"I hereby declare Presidential Decree Number 1737, otherwise known as The Public Order Act. This empowers me to issue orders as I, as President of the Republic of the Philippines, may deem necessary in order to clamp down on subversive publications or other media of mass communication and ban or regulate the holding of entertainment or exhibition deemed detrimental to the national interest. That, right there, is both an entertainment and an exhibition that is detrimental to the nation. Don't you all know that we have important things to take care of? The communists! The student activists! The militant farmers! These are real threats to the stability of our government.

"And so, with this presidential decree," Basti, or that Ferdinand, thunders on with words that would rival that sonic assault by the storm, "I hereby suspend your freedom of speech!"

The first to react to this is Mitzi who is holding her iPhone throughout this fucking crap called a presidential decree.

"President..." Mitzi reads aloud what she's typing, her fingers displaying a manual dexterity reserved for champion gamers and the assholes on Reddit and 4Chan, "Ferdinand...has...just...suspended...our...freedom...of...speech. Exclam, exclam, exclam, WTF, question mark, devil emoji."

Before Mitzi can pocket her phone, it vibrates and lights up screeches and comes alive like a fucking Decepticon.

She takes a moment before scrolling down the replies and says, "Same. Everyone thinks the same."

She seems disappointed as she flings her iPhone on the sofa.

"And what would that be?" I hear myself asking.

Mitzi aggregates all her replies, millions of them I am sure, that her single tweet has harvested from her fans that are hanging on to her every word. She spits this out via a single sentence.

"What is freedom of speech?"

This makes me think for a second.

Freedom of speech.

What is it, indeed?

Also.

Do we give a fuck if this freedom of speech is suspended?

Chapter Forty

D o I care if my freedom to post on my Insta is canceled?
Do I, like fuck!
Why is this even a fucking question?

———

Think of this, my lurves.

What @Basti, who is now Ferdinand, is saying is that all platforms need to be taken down.

And what if he has the bandwidth to do it?

No more TikTok. No more FB. No more Twitter. No more Insta. No more WhatsApp. No more Snapchat. No more Viber. No more Tumblr. No more Reddit. No more 8Chan. No more Ask.fm. No more Kik. No more Whisper. No more Twitch. No more Periscope. No more Pinterest. No more Patreon. No more PornHub. No more OnlyFans.

L'horreur!

@Basti, who is now Ferdinand, actually says that he is doing away with all the awesomeness in the world like some kind of dictator. Like some kind of tyrant.

He says something about making it his decree, what he terms "the suspension of our freedom of speech." The silly little heartbreaker is becoming a major fucking asshole.

And so of course, I take out my iPhone and update my feed. Yep, my lurves, on all my fucking socials.

"President Ferdinand has just suspended our freedom of speech!!! WTF?" I also add a devil emoji. Just to be on brand.

Now, I never expected that you, my lurves, are following my story in real-time as before I could even let go of my moi machine that is the latest iPhone on the market, it screams like a fucking beyatch in heat. The replies come flooding in.

And guess what, my lurves?

Not a single one of you fuckers know what freedom of speech is!

You all answered my post with a question.

"What is freedom of speech?"

I say this aloud just to fuck with @Basti, who is now Ferdinand.

And then he jumps right at moi.

Chapter Forty-One

Basti, or that Ferdinand, releases Vicente and jumps over to Mitzi before I can do any deep thinking about this fucking freedom of speech.

He grabs her from behind and uses his left hand to pin her to his chest.

Then, he uses his right hand to clamp down on her mouth.

Words, screams, sobs, and pleas for help from Mitzi are muffled until they come down to a complete silence.

Every one of us holds our breath.

It is one thing when Basti, or that Ferdinand, pins down Vicente, that retard.

It is a totally different thing when he does it to Mitzi.

Mitzi, my beautiful Mitzi who is afraid, unmoving, helpless.

This gruesome sight renders us speechless.

That's right, we are all speechless as fuck.

I don't really know what freedom of speech is, but I can feel that it is being taken away.

Everyone, and everything, freezes.

The entire penthouse is now a life-sized high school

diorama project of a group of fucking useless fucks who does not have a single clue as to what to do.

Outside, the storm intensifies.

I can hear the wind howling like wolves. Like witches.

Bursts of lightning fork down from the heavens. Or surge up from hell below.

Cracks of thunder follow.

A perfect soundtrack to the crime being committed inside the room.

Pia breaks the stillness.

Contrary to what I expect, it is not an attack on her former BFF, my other one true love, my BAE, my Mitzi. There is neither hatred nor vengeance in her words.

And get this.

What Pia says could have been the sanest thing ever spoken that night.

"This is fucking stupid," Pia says. "Whoever knows how to pray should say the words now. Literally. For realz."

See?

Muy bien, Pia!

Isn't that the best idea ever spoken this Friday night? Genius, if I may say so.

Except that it beggars the fucking question as to who should utter the incantation and articulate the intercession.

Also, what kind of prayer. I think a Hail Mary is not gonna cut it tonight.

As are the words "I compel thee!"

These are very potent words by Hollywood standards, but I don't think these will work against that Ferdinand. I recall his earlier words of establishing a dictatorship, a monarchy even, and I wonder if ever a prayer, any prayer at all, has worked in bringing these down.

The most that prayers could do is help you pass a board

exam, right? And even then, you would still have to review and score yourself a cheat sheet.

So, no, I seriously doubt that saying a prayer can topple governments, irresponsible, oppressive governments. Or the fucking monarchy.

So, here's what I do.

I volunteer Pia.

Based purely on how she was so eager to cross herself earlier before all this shit started.

"Do it, Pia," I say. "You are our only hope. Say a prayer for us. Now."

Understanding that, ummm, time is becoming of the essence, Pia shoots me a reply.

"Me?" Pia says. "Me? Ohhheeemgeee! My head literally exploded! I can't even! I won't even! I have forgotten how to even! There is no way I could even! I...like...no!"

Upon hearing this, Basti, or that Ferdinand, loosens his grip on Mitzi.

But he doesn't let her go, not just yet.

Vicente then volunteers. Fuck me, but the retard really volunteers. Although, I shit you not, stranger things are still to come.

"Vicente is willing to do it," Vicente says. "Vicente can say the prayer. A Hail Mary, right? Three of them, maybe?"

Well. As it turns out, Vicente is a very protective man but whether it is for Basti's sake or for Pia, we will never know.

And what he has just uttered is not just a suggestion, either.

The retard actually starts doing the Hail Mary, all mangled of course, even saying the last line three times like a chorus.

"Pray for us sinners, now and at the hour of our death, Amen. Pray for us sinners, now and at the hour of our death,

Amen. Pray for us sinners, now and at the hour of our death, Amen."

It does nothing. As I have expected.

Basti is still possessed by that Ferdinand who seems to be getting more menacing by the second.

"You do it," Pia says, looking at me.

For the first time I get the vibe that she is actually seeing me. That I exist. That I matter enough in her life.

This is way beyond the half-meant "How's life?" that I always answer with "Same shit, different day."

Now we are having a very different kind of shit on what could have been a same-old, same-old Friday.

"Rafa," Pia pleads again. "You know a thing or two about prayers, right? With your Grandpa and all? Please. Say a prayer, Rafa. Any prayer."

There is a certain kind of desperation that she tries very hard—and fails very miserably—to hide.

I don't wanna do it. Believe you me.

I really never.

Wanna.

Do.

It.

But another muffled scream comes from my other only love, my Mitzi.

Something that sounds like, "Rafa?"

Yes, my name spoken both as a command and a promise.

And so of course...

Here's the fucking thing.

I don't do prayers.

Don't even know the words to "Our Father," much more than "Hail Mary."

As a direct descendant of the former *Arsobispo de Manila*, you would expect that prayer and all things pious would be in my blood. But no, Sir.

Because my *erpats* grew up in a very religious household, he sort of sheltered me from all that crap. From crosses and communions to bibles and baptisms. Yes, I don't even know if I was ever baptized much more got confirmed.

But.

But...

But!

Someone has to pray to the Dark Lord.

Chapter Forty-Two

Rafa prays to the Dark Lord.

But Rafa does it the way only he can do it.

To mean that he did not exactly jump at the chance to save *moi* from being strangled by @Basti, who is now Ferdinand.

Yep, my lurves, I am being restrained by the major asshole formerly known as that silly little heartbreaker. Against my will, obvs. I say buh-bye to any spanking or any other BDSM play. Silently, of course as my mouth is clamped shut. I try to shout and scream and cry. Nothing doing. Not only is there no safe word, I am also on fucking mute.

And it looks like everyone else is, too. No one moves. No one speaks. They too, are on fucking mute like a Zoom meet gone bonkers.

All I hear is the fucking storm that is still gathering strength and pounding the penthouse like it is singularly focused on getting in and crashing our little party.

Lightning forks down from the heavens. So bright that even the whiteness of the room is taken up a notch. Any cinematographer would have had a boner seeing how bright every fucking thing is. Light captured at 60 fps. Pure Ultra HD 4K awesome-

ness. Broadcast quality brilliance, already color corrected, graded, and edited.

And then the thunder comes. A series of explosions in Dolby Atmos and when I say surround sound, I fucking mean that I am surrounded by sound. Deep and precise and coming from above and also from below, to my left and to my right, with fucking bass and treble and all the other trimmings that could only come from being professionally processed on ProTools.

Yep, I know all these for how else would I stand out among the many other online strippers, ooops, excusez-moi, content creators, on OnlyFans? Quality content is key. And so are equipment and editing and the whole thing termed as production value.

Anyhoo.

All of us are frozen like a livestream that stops buffering midway and the only way to move shit forward is to reboot the fucking router.

Then @Pia speaks.

Well.

Credit where credit is due.

The adorable little slut actually has an idea.

And the idea is that someone should pray to the Dark Lord.

"For realz," @Pia says.

Très bien, I say to myself.

And get this my lurves, Rafa does not come to my rescue upon hearing this suggestion.

As per yoozh.

On the contrary, Rafa volunteers @Pia to lead the prayer.

And this is when I realize that we are almost back to our normal programming. Except for @Basti, who is now Ferdinand, everyone is acting their part.

Rafa being Rafa bouncing the suggestion right back to @Pia.

And @Pia being @Pia flat out refusing. Because, she can't even.

And @Vicente being @Vicente volunteering for a reason only god knows what.

Again, credit where credit is due.

Hey, choosers cannot be beggars the way beggars cannot be choosers, so no one objects to the spirit of sacrifice being offered by that lousy little retard @Vicente.

A prayer is a prayer and who really cares who says it as long as it does the fucking job.

Except what @Vicente utters is not in the vein of ABSVRDVM PASSWORDVM but something that would surely disappoint Sister Heidi.

Are you ready, my lurves?

"Pray for us sinners, now and at the hour of death, Amen. Pray for us sinners, now and at the hour of death, Amen. Pray for us sinners, now and at the hour of death, Amen."

Yep, three fucking times.

But it is not a charm.

And neither did it work

In the meantime, @Basti, who is now Ferdinand, is still all over me and not in a good way. My mouth is still clamped shut and my body is still immobilized. So much for my freedom of speech.

"Rafa?"

That's right, my lurves.

A command and a promise rolled into one.

The very same thing that, once upon a happier time, made me do things to Rafa once. Maybe twice. K, maybe even more.

"Rafa?"

I say it.

With my eyes.

"Rafa?"

And guess what?

Rafa receives the message loud and clear.

And so, in his own way, Rafa utters a prayer.

Here's the thing.

It might come as a bit of a surprise to you, my lurves, but prayers are not really my shit. Swear to gods, hope to die. Prayers are the last refuge of the scoundrel and moi is everything but a scoundrel. I've never prayed in high school, never prayed in that finishing school abroad, never prayed inside a church. I just don't see the point. Because really, what could I possibly say to my god and influence her in my favor?

Ask Sister Heidi.

The only time I ever say god's name is when I am on the throes of my very own la petite mort, and even then, I say her name in lowercase g.

Then again, I am willing to try everything at least once, maybe even twice, so why not this thing they call a prayer?

Even if it is to the Dark Lord.

Time for some original content.

And so, in my own way, I also say a prayer.

I close my eyes.

And in my mind, I utter a string of words. My very own incantation, invocation, and intentions that I can only hope will be verified, accepted, and pass any and all authentication protocols set up by Beelzebub and cut through to the military-grade 256-bit encryption that secures all the malevolence of hell below.

I do my own version of ABSVRDVM PASSWORDVM.

I hope.

And I pray.

And I believe.

I utter these words.
GIGANTVM ASSHOLVM.
GIGANTVM RETARDVM.
GIGANTVM SLVTVM.
CANCELVM CVLTVRVM.
LITERALVM DEADVM.
I know. I know.
What the actual fuck?
Well, well, well, my lurves.

It is at this point in my awesome story that I throw the content creation workflow out the floor-to-ceiling window.

I pivot like I have never pivoted before.

Chapter Forty-Three

A nd it is at this point in our little story that we make another turn. If this is a novel, we now head into Act 3.

As this is a different kind of story, we are going to fire the loaded gun that wasn't even introduced in Act 1.

We are going into the final reversal.

Shit is going to level up from a what-the-fuck to oh-my-fucking-gods.

And it all starts with my prayer.

As I have already made clear, I don't do prayers.

No one has taught me how to pray. Not at home, not at school. And in the few and far between times that I've been inside a church, you know the drill—weddings, baptisms, funerals—I just went with the flow, kneeling when the rest of the congregation kneeled, doing the Amen when I heard it, bouncing back the peace-be-with-you when it was directed my way.

And so, to bastardize Frankie baby, I pray it my way.

I pray to the Dark Lord as earnestly as I can muster after doing the sign of the inverted cross.

I sling a few intentions towards my friends.

Without even uttering a single word out loud.

But.

But...

But!

I am thinking of my very own made-up words in my very own dead as fuck language.

Little did I know that, as the night deepens, my own dead language will become a romance language. But patience, my friends. This shit will be explained later.

Meanwhile, I say, in my head, the following words:

GIGANTVM ASSHOLVM.

GIGANTVM RETARDVM.

GIGANTVM SLVTVM.

CANCELVM CVLTVRVM.

LITERALVM DEADVM.

And it all feels real.

Like I am connecting with another being.

Like I am having an internal conversation with a higher power.

And just like any conversation, after I say my piece, I get a reply.

And this is when things start getting really, really, really fucked up.

Total darkness descends.

Solid and absolute.

This blackness is stabbed by the brightest flash of lightning I have ever seen.

Sharp and cutting.

And then thunder comes. Of fucking course, it does.

It is maddening as fuck.

When the power comes back on, the whole place is darker than before. A veil of shadows covers everything. Everyone is reduced to a silhouette.

And then I hear myself speak.

"Whereas, on the basis of carefully evaluated and verified information, it is definitely established that lawless elements who are moved by a common or similar ideological conviction, design, strategy and goal, and enjoying the active moral and material support of a foreign power and being guided and directed by intensely devoted, well trained, determined and ruthless groups of men seeking refuge under the protection of our constitutional liberties to promote and attain their ends, have entered into a conspiracy and have in fact joined and banded their resources and forces together for the prime purpose of, and in fact they have been and are actually staging, undertaking and waging an armed insurrection and rebellion against the Government of the Republic of the Philippines in order to forcibly seize political and state power in this country, overthrow the duly constituted government, and supplant our existing political, social, economic and legal order with an entirely new one whose form of government, whose system of laws, whose conception of God and religion, whose notion of individual rights and family relations, and whose political, social, economic, legal and moral precepts are based on the Marxist-Leninist-Maoist teachings and beliefs..."

Who would have thought, amirite?
Marxist-Leninist-Maoist, my ass.
Yes, that Ferdinand is grabbing me by the fucking balls.

Now, I am going to spare you with the rest of that fucking speech.

Because it is boring as fuck.

First, there's a lot of "Whereases," around 23 I believe.

Second, there's a lot of big words, too. Like "Writ of Habeas Corpus," and "Resurgence of the Communist Threat," and "Lenin's Idea of a Swift, Armed Uprising," and "Mao's Concept of a Protracted People's War."

And third, get this. There are even bigger words than those. Yes, believe you me. Ginormous words like "*Hukbong Magpapalaya ng Bayan*," and "*Lapiang Manggagawa*," and "*Malayang Samahan ng mga Magsasaka*," and "*Kabataang Makabayan*," and "*Samahang Demokratiko ng Kabataan*."

See? How can anybody FB or tweet or 'gram that shit?

So.

What I am going to do is fast forward to the ending of that speech.

Are you ready?

Here goes...

I speak again.

"Now, therefore, I, Ferdinand E. Marcos, President of the Philippines, by virtue of the powers vested upon me by Article VII, Section 10, Paragraph 2 of the Constitution, do hereby place the entire Philippines as defined in Article I, Section 1 of the Constitution under Martial Law, and in my capacity as their Commander-in-Chief, do hereby command the Armed Forces of the Philippines, to maintain law and order throughout the Philippines, prevent or suppress all forms of lawless violence as well as any act of insurrection or rebellion and to enforce obedience to all the laws and decrees, orders and regulations promulgated by me personally or upon my direction.

"In addition, I do hereby order that all persons presently

detained, as well as all others who may hereafter be similarly detained for the crimes of insurrection or rebellion, and all other crimes and offenses committed in furtherance or on the occasion thereof, or incident thereto, or in connection therewith, for crimes against national security and the law of nations, crimes against public order, crimes involving usurpation of authority, rank, title, and improper use of names, uniforms and insignia, crimes committed by public officers, and for such other crimes as will be enumerated in orders that I shall subsequently promulgate, as well as crimes as a consequence of any violation of any decree, order or regulation promulgated by me personally or promulgated upon my direction shall be kept under detection until otherwise ordered released by me or my duly designated representative.

"In witness whereof, I have hereunto set my hand and caused the seal of the Republic of the Philippines to be affixed.

"Done in the City of Manila, this 21st day of September, in the Year of Our Lord, nineteen hundred and seventy-two."

Now that feels like a fucking Friday, amirite?!

Chapter Forty-Four

Finally, a fucking Friday.
    Fridaaaaaaaaaaaaaayyy!
    My me day!
This is all going to be about moi!
I am going to author myself like I have never authored myself before.
I know, I know.
It might sound a bit sus, but remember that this is my story.
And that the content creation workflow has long since been thrashed, deleted, and purged.
Think of this unexpected awesomeness as me newsjacking my very own story, retargeting all of you my lurves to an even more interactive content. Oh, fuck yes, every single one of you motherfuckers will interact like you've never interacted before. You will engage like you have never engaged before. You will fucking learn like you've never learned before.
To move this shit forward, think of what I am going to tell you as no longer ephemeral content but a real story. Fuck anals and algos, metrics and measures, KPIs and ROIs. I am now telling my story without giving a fuck to the numbers and the bean counters.

What is now happening is free from the tyranny of the likes and the mentions, the hearts and the shares, the comments and the quotes.

Yes, my lurves, shit's getting real AF!

And this awesomeness that is this new reality starts in darkness.

But first, a throwback Thursday to end all throwback Thursdays.

And by this, I mean yesterday.

Yesterday when everything was peachy.

It all started with an alert on my iPhone that my moolah is not in fucking order. I have an overdraft in one of my checking accounts and when I opened the app, I find out that indeed, I am in major monetary debt. I sneak a peek at my savings accounts in three different banks and what's staring at me on all financial fronts is the number zero. Now add that to the overdraft and the correct answer is that my finances are in the fucking negative. No, my lurves, that's not girl math. That's real math. Everything is automated when it comes to handling the revenues from all my socials via the payment gateways PayPal, Square, and Stripe, so this bankruptcy is not an error, human or otherwise. I am not raking in the fucking moolah. Not from my vlogging, not from my styling, not from my fucking myself on OnlyFans. I am broke as fuck. And in debt. As in I can't even afford a fucking burger from Mickey Ds. This is worse than that time in Switzerland. Being broke is paradise compared to being locked square in the sights of a bank for estafa. Yep, my lurves, there is no money to manage, but oh, there's a lot to talk about the lack of it. My lack of it. Like how will I ever survive? By my beauty? By my brains? And it's not like I can just jet my way to the Middle East for some quick buck as Arabs are not into non-virgins. Google it if you think I am bullshitting you. And it's not like I can just

give a call to 'Gette for a fucking bailout. She is also out of
funds. Add to that, we're long past that point of speaking to
each other the moment she saw one of my artfully curated vids,
ooops, amateur porn. Mothers, right my lurves?

And speaking of not speaking to ma famille, I also cannot
have a word with Gio. In the literal sense as that philanderer
has just had a stroke while on the receiving end of a blowjob
that rewired half of his DOM body. Looks like too much teeth
unleashed on the shaft at the wrong second can electrify the
whole nervous system and fry the brain. He no longer has any
control of his mouth and his penis and his anus as well as the
left extremities. It almost looks sad, seeing him fed through a
fucking tube and attired in diapers. At least the nurse is a cutie,
one of those porny ones who still wear stockings in this day and
age like that evil nurse on Netflix. But this beauty needs to be
warned that hitching her wagon on a has-been trapo being
chased by a dozen mistresses won't be a ticket to a comfortable
life. Especially if that invalid trapo has hitched his wagon on
the wrong political party that is sure to lose big time in the
upcoming elections. What good is the salvation business when
one can't even save one's self? The fucking irony.

Well.

As a consolation prize, I still have my lurvelife.

Ha! Who the fuck am I kidding?

I have long ago ghosted the one and only lurve of my life,
Rafa, whose innocence I willingly defiled in one unforgettable
marathon fucking session that still makes me blush whenever I
think about it today. That fucker actually made me cum. Once.
And twice. K, even thrice. K, even more. We even have that
inside joke, remember? Rafa is the reason I do not have a BAE
and maybe will never have one ever again. It's totes adorbs and
also sad as fuck. Of course, it's not him, it's me. This much I
know. Yep, I am just a girl who has walked away from a boy
and fucked up the chance at that one true lurve. See, Rafa was
the one that I made sure got away. There is just no way that

after taking away his virginity, I would also take away his future. He is no oil Sheikh, no agented footballer, not even a CEO, but fuck it, he is Rafa and my Swiss education is not just cut out for him. His being average, ordinary, and everyday is so adorbs to behold that it hurts as fuck. He's got a life and a real one that is totally free from the preening and the posturing in front of a camera and I am not about to fuck that one up. Sure, I have had my own share of fucking horrible people up—not to mention despicable brands—and canceling their presence on social media but I just wouldn't do it to Rafa. I won't dox him or troll him or swat him or flame him. I just wouldn't. How's that for true lurve? This is the one reason I wouldn't even let him friend me. And have blocked every single one of his subscription attempts on my PornHub and OnlyFans. Keeping Rafa as a friend, a fan, a follower would just continue breaking my heart and messing up my head. I know, I know, I am the one who has ghosted Rafa but given the choice, I would rather that he was the one who has ghosted me. For then I could at least live with myself instead of living a lie. Oh, Rafa! How could I possibly have fucked this one up?

Before yesterday magically dissolved into this Friday like a seamless edit, I reached out to my friends. Well, my so-called friends and asked if anyone of them would like to get high with me. But no one answered. There were no takers. Not even premium cocaine can bait any of these fuckers to hang out with me. And this, on a fucking Thursday night.

Three minutes to midnight, I went to the pool and dipped my toes into the warm, waiting waters as I took a drag from my other poison of choice, Marl red, not thinking about my non-life. I snorted from my stash, using the webbing in between the thumb and forefinger of my left hand and rubbed the few precious morsels of the snow on my upper gums. Sweet release comes as only being pleasured by unadulterated snow can come.

Pure bliss.

Everything is peachy.

I've no money, no family, no friends.

I finished my smoke and flicked the smoldering stub towards the deep end of the pool where I saw the sign on one of the tiles.

12 FEET.

It would be all too easy.

This early checkout.

Live fast, die young, and leave a beautiful corpse, right my lurves? That would be fucking hardcore. Being unalive via your own very hands.

When was suicide ever not cool?

Besides, how cool would it be if I ghosted my very own self?

I took a look at my reflection in the pool and saw a very beautiful human staring back at me.

Right then, I realized one truth.

All I've got is me.

Which means my youth.

Which, in this age of curated content that drives the attention economy into a trillion-dollar industry, is still a very valuable currency.

Yep, that's a beauty right there, looking back at me. A real beauty unfiltered by Lensa and unretouched by Facetune.

And then I remember. In just a few breaths, it would already be Friday.

My me day.

It's all going to be all about moi.

Friday. Inside @Basti's crib. On a stormy night.

Once more, the entire world is baptized in absolute blackness.

Something dark and alive and evil smothers us all as every light source on this sweet decaying Earth is extinguished.

To bastardize Sister Heidi, "Let there be dark. And there was dark."

Yes, my lurves, you might be thinking that it is just a power outage being caused by this fucking storm, but no.

Like the silence, this darkness is alive.

And it has a tongue.

Even more disturbing, this darkness has teeth.

And it is eating its way into me.

Inside of me.

I am getting devoured alive.

———

Self-authorship is self-trafficking is self-actualization.

Except that while I feel myself being trafficked and actualized, I am no longer the author of this story.

My story.

Something, or someone, is inside me.

There is no more Marie Celine Gallofin Ricafort.

No more Mitzi.

No more @Mitzi.

I, the—fuck this word—influencer of all influencers, is getting influenced.

And I fucking lurve it.

———

As the light comes back on that does very little to push the darkness out, I hear Rafa speak.

He is using these ginormous words "therefore" and "hereby" and "in witness whereof."

You guessed it right, my lurves.

Rafa is now being possessed by that fucker, Ferdinand.

And now he is declaring, in his very own words, "Martial Law."

*Of course, I have no idea what this Martial Law means but
I lurve it.*

I super lurve it.

*I am getting the vibe that it would be the awesomest ever!
Martial Law!*

Chapter Forty-Five

Martial Law, baby!

I am in full Presidential mode as I go dictatorial on their privileged, self-entitled, coño fucking asses!

———

Being Ferdinand, I really have no choice. I have to save this fucking republic. And with the current situation, I have to reform the social, economic, and political institutions of our great country.

———

Ha! Who the fuck am I kidding?

I declared Martial Law because I have the power to silence those who need to be silenced. To disappear those who need to be disappeared. To murder those who need to be murdered.

This is very important because only if the dissenters are

silenced can I continue to plunder the nation's almost unlimited wealth.

Oh, fuck yes, we as a nation, are wealthy. Believe you me.

Some say we are second only to Japan but even that shit is debatable.

You want proof?

Let me give you three.

And I am not talking about the fucking Gross Domestic Product. Or Per Capita Income. Or Capital Output Ratio. These are just numbers that could be manipulated and misinterpreted.

Also, no one gives a shit about these things.

However.

My three reasons as to why we are wealthy and the greatest ever are cold, hard facts.

One, our republic is the only Asian nation that has a direct flight to the United States and vice versa.

Two, we have discotheques. Discotheques!

And do you really want to go to point number three?

Okay, three. We don't have a Yoko Ono.

There, there, and there.

The Republic of the Philippines, soon to be the Kingdom of Maharlika, is the greatest nation on this side of the Orient of this beautiful green Earth.

And I, of course, the President and soon-to-be King, am the greatest leader on this side of the Pacific.

Now, who are these dissenters to say otherwise?

Ha! Got you there again, haven't I?

I declared Martial Law because I finally got the chance to cancel every single one of these useless motherfuckers.

And by cancel, I mean the analog kind.

The kind that involves pain and suffering.

The kind that involves death and dying.

But going back to this Friday night.

This night I am the motherfucking President of the Republic of the Philippines.

This night I am a strongman.

This night I am Ferdinand.

What I see before me are young dissenters.

Barely out of their teens, these fuckers and fuckerettes.

What Rizal has termed "The Hope of the Fatherland," although I am sure that this idea is lost on their coke-addled minds. More like "The Dope of the Fatherland."

Despite the Martial Law that I have just declared, they are trying in earnest to destabilize the government.

They are already a very serious threat to my presidency.

How serious, you ask?

Well.

How about every single one of these fuckers and fuckerettes pretending not to recognize me?

Me!

President Ferdinand Emmanuel Edralin Marcos, Sr.!

These ignorant fuckers keep calling me Rafa!

Like, "Come back to us Rafa!"

And "Rafa, don't do this man."

And "Rafa, please, you have to stop this shit."

And "Vicente thinks Rafa is just trying very hard to be funny."

Yes, not a single person in the room addressed me as "His Excellency."

Yes.

Got you there again.

These pathetic little fucks do not even recognize me as Rafa.

The Rafa that they have canceled because I just wasn't cool enough. Or loaded enough. Or whatever the fuck it is that I need to be one of them, these—fuck this word —influencers.

The Rafa that was their biggest fan.

Yep.

I was their biggest fan.

Not just in that stupid Insta but in real life.

Well, this biggest fan is about to become a fucking Stan!

And so I do my Commander-in-Chief thing.

Now, kindly allow me to tell you this.

Being Commander-in-Chief is the best part of being President, especially if you are the greatest resistance leader during World War II, as well as the most decorated soldier who ever served in the United States Army.

Okay, let's please not talk about the alleged fakery of all my war medals, how they were all manufactured by the finest craftsmen in all of Recto.

I am sure that these stupid fucks—I finally get their names thanks to my prodigious memory that helped me top the bar exam from the written part to the oral examinations—Mitzi, Pia, Basti, and that retard who calls himself Vicente, have never heard about a perfect crime.

Or, even more important, that I have committed the perfect crime.

We all know what a perfect crime is, don't we?

But still, a refresher.

A crime is perfect when everybody knows who committed the crime but no one can prove that the known criminal committed that crime.

It is a very safe assumption to say that these stupid fuckers have no idea how a certain individual named Julio Nalundasan once existed on the face of this sweet green Earth.

And how, on the very same day he won a governmental seat against my father in a Congressional election, I wiped this individual off this planet.

Forever.

I canceled this Nalundasan motherfucker the analog way.

With a fucking gun.

Ah, the weight of the pistol!

The sound of the report!

The kick of the recoil!

I could never forget that murder as it is the one thing that launched my political career.

Of course, they, my father's political opponents, thought that they had me then.

But.

But...

But!

Being convicted, imprisoned, and then set free again makes that crime even more perfect than it already is.

Oh, fuck yes, I have committed a crime so perfect that it is beyond compare, it is beyond *beyond* to this very day.

And I plan on doing it again.

And this time, I am taking it to the next level.

This time, I am committing a double murder.

Again.

Chapter Forty-Six

Again.

Let me repeat, my lurves, that I am totes magotes onboard with Rafa.

My Rafa.

Who is now Ferdinand.

Who is now into cancel culture.

Yep, someone who calls the hashtag a pound sign is planning to ruin us all. Someone who can't even define KPI is willing to fuck us all. Someone who can't even do a proper Insta post is strategizing to cancel us all.

I know, I know.

A bit sus of moi to be now in agreement with Rafa, who used to be my BAE, the very same one that I made sure got away.

But then again, I really have no choice.

Because—fuck this word—influencing.

Have you ever heard of Influencers in the Wild?

My lurves! That one is truth. Or gospel to channel my inner Sister Heidi.

Head over there as soon as you have subscribed to my OnlyFans and see for yourself how the influencing sausage is *made. Take a peek behind the 'grammable curtains and see firsthand all the innards and discards, all the bloody bits and shitty bags, all the putrid shots and the perverted drafts that have fallen on the greasy, grimy, and rancid creation floor of social media platforms only to be picked up, wiped off, and reworked back into the slimy casing of social media and marketed as content. Getting down and dirty, while not a guarantee for success, is part and parcel of the influencing biz.*

Yep, my lurves, there are a million untold stories of the great lengths I have to go through for that perfect shot, that immortal line, that unforgettable pose.

There is not a single thing in the world that I would not do to keep my—fuck this word—influence.

Much more on this very Friday when I am already under the influence.

And that would include Martial Law.

———

Anyhoo.

This Martial Law thing.

I hear Rafa, poor, sad Rafa who is now Ferdinand, speak.

And he starts his speech with the word "Whereas."

But get this. He is totally on message.

And the message is this: that he knows he is being canceled.

Fuck me sideways, my lurves.

Nothing could be truer than that message.

Well, of course, his verbiage is not really 'grammable, much more heartable, or even sharable but this fucker knows his shit.

Like the words "Marxist-Leninist-Maoist."

Or these: "armed insurrection and rebellion."

Or even: "Kabataang Makabayan" and "Samahang Demokratiko ng Kabataan."

See? Crypto as fuck. Creepy as fuck. How can one even tweet this shit?

And then again, he is on message.

Here's the thing my lurves.

Are you ready?

I totally get this message.

But wait, there's more.

Rafa, who is now Ferdinand, is about to get even weirder like he has never weirded us before.

He utters some crap about protecting this great republic. To mean his own brand. He knows that he better cancel everyone before he himself gets canceled. Now, how woke is that?

This Martial Law is nothing but cancel culture gone wild. If this is a treatment in one of my pre-prods, I would term it as Dystopian meets Dickensian. With all the grime and the grit associated with these words. End of the world scenario, like, you know, the Book of fucking Revelations. That weeping and gnashing of teeth, that rending of garments, that cursing to the high heavens. Death, the Beast, and the bottomless pit.

Again, thanks to Sister Heidi for my favorite quote from le Bible, this passage from Revelations chapter 9, verse 6:

"And in those days shall men seek death, and shall not find it; and shall desire to die, and death shall flee from them."

In the pervading darkness, the very same darkness that is alive and eating its way into my very being, I can feel that Rafa, who is now Ferdinand, is planning murder. He is doing the math and coming up with his own equation on how to arrive at the value of his very own X.

X = Death.

Death = the ultimate cancel.

And here I come to the fucking rub.

I am not going to have myself canceled.

Self-authorship is self-trafficking is self-actualization is self-preservation.

And this self-realization is as bright as the lightning that is forking down from the heavens as if god herself wants to join us on this awesomeness that is this Friday.

Chapter Forty-Seven

L ightning.
    Thunder.
    Very, very exciting.
Darkness descends upon the room once again, the kind that lingers in your head, the kind that freezes the marrow in your bones.

When the light returns, the room is cloaked in a gauze of gloom. The shadows are sharp. The silhouettes are deceitful.

And yet.

And yet...

And yet I can see very clearly.

———

There is no question as to who these two subversives that need to die tonight are.

One is that asshole Basti, who, strangely enough, feels like a brother to me. Like we have the same belief, the same principles, like we even went to the same school. I am getting the sense that our paths just took different turns. And that at any other time, we could have been lording over this great country together as its leaders. That feeling that he knows me on a personal level, and that I also do of him.

Yes, that saying about keeping your friends close and your enemies closer comes to mind.

Maybe this is the reason why this asshole is so belligerent, as if toppling down my rule is his one and only mission in life.

That Basti is one dangerous fucker and must be stopped.

Now, what would make this crime perfect of course is that somebody must be framed for committing Basti's murder.

Someone unknown.

Someone dispensable.

A nobody, basically.

And the perfect candidate would be...drum roll, please...

That retard Vicente.

Yes, that weird little shit who refers to himself in the third person.

Well, tonight, Vicente is about to witness Vicente get murdered.

As I plan this, I start feeling my manhood get real hard.

As in really, really hard.

Blood is pulsing through my veins, commanding all my senses to be alert as when that famous whodunit in the international airport that bears my name was committed.

But this time, instead of Aquino-Galman, it's going to be The Basti-Vicente Double Murder Case, yet another perfect entry into the Annals of Unsolved Crimes of the 21st Century.

As my erection becomes unbearably massive, I adjust my manhood.

Pia sees the whole thing.

Me.

And my hand.

In my pants.

Calibrating my bursting Presidential penis.

"Ohhheeemgeee!" Pia says. "My head just literally exploded! Is he nursing a boner? I am getting all the feelz! Literally! For realz! Look, Mitzi! Look! That is one ginormous erection! What I would do to give it a very slow fap until it fucking cums!"

Now, I don't know and I don't give a fuck about these spoiled brats and bitches but the way they care about the English language speaks volumes.

A lesson is most certainly in order.

Mitzi—the other girl who, to be honest, looks just like my Meldy—whips out her iPhone.

She snaps a photo of my enormous Presidential erection, my *membrvm virilvm*, and says that it is going to be my profile picture.

"Ferdinand needs to be on FB, Pia," Mitzi says. "Insta and TikTok, and Twitter too. And the rest of the socials in the aether. And...done!

"Hello @Ferdy!

"Welcome to the real word! I am so gonna friend and follow you! Maybe you can even guest me on my OnlyFans!"

———

All this time, Basti is talking with Vicente.

Yes, in blatant disregard of my Martial rule.

The very same law that I have, mere minutes before, personally signed, pronounced, and executed.

Vicente, like the retard that he is, engages himself into the conversation.

These two are hatching a plan.

An ill-conceived plan that will arrive stillborn any moment now.

I walk over to Basti and before he can react, I give him a mighty slap and pull out the pistol tucked in the waistband of his pants.

If there is one thing I learned from being a dictator, it is this: introduce a gun to any situation and the dynamic radically changes.

Of course, it is ideal that you should be the one handling the fucking gun.

Like I am doing this stormy Friday night.

The look of surprise comes unbidden from everyone, with Basti being the most unbelieving of them all.

Surprise, surprise.

A gun.

And it is in my hand.

A gun.

This is the one and only reason why Basti was so eager to open the safe inside his bedroom when I plundered his wealth and pillage his cash including his emergency money all still bound by the *Bangko Sentral* seal earlier.

Basti was clueless that I saw him take the gun lying by the meticulously arranged bricks of cash as furtively as he could manage.

A gun.

I grip it within my right hand and the heft feels reassuring.

Out of habit, I check it for bullets.

Yes, the gun is fully loaded.

And, get this, it is a .22 of all things.

My favorite piece of hardware.

Whoever sold this analog killing machine to Basti knows what he is doing, he really does.

"Vicente doesn't even know you have a gun, Basti," Vicente, in all of his third-person lunacy, says.

"Of course, I have a fucking gun," Basti spits out his reply. With his words come blood and saliva. He adds, pointing to me, "Rafa sold it to me. I belong to their preferred roster of fucking clientele!"

iPhones suddenly start blinking and bawling and vibrating like the apocalypse is upon us.

Basti, with the gun still pointed at him, flinches as if I have just squeezed the trigger.

Vicente swallows whatever it is that he wants to say.

Mitzi opens her iPhone as Pia looks on.

"Unreal," Mitzi says. "You guys would not fucking believe this. 41 million comments. 43 million likes. And 47 million follower requests and counting. That's the entire Philippines on social media right there. @Ferdy is totally happening. @Ferdy is totally lit. @Ferdy is totally trending. @Ferdy is hot as fuck.

"Well, with these digits, I am so gonna have him do a version two point oh of my *brokenvm hymenvm!* My god, that *gigantvm penisivm* must be so deleeesh!

"Not just once, but maybe twice! Livestreamed on my OnlyFans! Think of the likes! The comments! The hearts! The fucking dollars!"

I interpret that to mean that I am popular in their world,

this, despite the undisputable fact that no one really knows me, not even these four persons in this very room I find myself now.

And it's all thanks to my massive Presidential erection.

And also that Mitzi, yes, the one who looks just like my Meldy, wants to have a taste of my Presidential cum and wants to fuck me to kingdom come.

Mitzi pauses and weirdly enough, even the fucking storm unleashes a ceasefire. Stillness descends as even breaths are held.

That is until Mitzi continues with, "Now updating my relationship status to 'It's complicated.' Broken heart emoji. Done!"

Likes.

Comments.

Hearts.

What the fuck are these?

Well, I've got a few numbers of my own.

How about 3,247 murdered?

Or, over 40,000 tortured?

Or, over 60,000 illegally detained?

And my personal favorite, the number of the disappeared, so unknowable that, to quote that Pia, "I can't even..."

But.

But...

But!

If these are not impressive enough, I have this magic number.

10.

As in 10 billion.

As in 10 billion American dollars.

––––––––

Now, kindly allow me to break this narrative for a moment so we can think about this.

10. Billion. American dollars.

Let us not debate how I got it.

The idea here is that I've got it.

That's my wealth.

That's my worth.

That's my world.

Chew on that for a second.

Because these fuckers and fuckerettes—these fucking influencers whose life is devoted to monetizing the minutia of the pathetic empty existence they try very hard to convince themselves is a life—will never fucking get it.

––––––––

10 fucking billion American dollars!

This is what is at stake here.

If this Friday is a novel, this would be my character motivation.

I will do anything, everything, for this amount.

What is the suspension of the Freedom of Speech compared to that?

Or the declaration of Martial Law?

Or even the execution of a double murder?

Chapter Forty-Eight

A fter all the doublethink about Martial Law and the doubletalk about protecting this great republic, Rafa, who is now Ferdinand, is going for the doublefuck.
He is, totes magotes, going for a double murder.
And it is going to be double deleeesh.

What's also deleeesh AF?
His gigantvm penisivm!
But credit where credit is due. It is actually @Pia, that adorable little slut, who spies his massive erection.
And when I say massive erection, I mean a massive erection.
Like one of those cards in the game Cards Against Humanity that @Basti has introduced us to many Fridays ago, Rafa, who is now Ferdinand, inserts his right hand inside his selvage pants and adjusts his raging peen, except that there is no attempt at concealing his boner.
@Pia, as expected, squeals like the adorable little slut that she is. About how she is getting "all the feelz" and "for realz,"

and how her head "literally exploded." Yep, my lurves, right in front of @Basti her BAE, and @Vicente, the dude she is banging on the side, she declares that she wants a taste of that massive erection.

And who can blame her?

Even I am getting moist.

And so I do what I do best.

I whip out my iPhone and snap a pic of that gigantvm penisivm demanding to break free from the confines of that very tight denim that is holding it prisoner.

Because pics or didn't happen, right, my lurves?

And also, that massive erection is a work of art that must be immortalized.

I've seen a lot of dicks, fondled a lot of dicks, sucked a lot of dicks, fucked a lot of dicks but nothing compares to that pulsating, raging manhood before me in terms of length and girth and balls.

I get my framing right, my lighting right, my filter right, and I snap a shot.

Then I do another shot.

I choose the best among the two and then edit its exposure, brilliance, highlights, the yoozh, and after saving it, upload this perfection of a photo as a profile pic.

Of Rafa, who is now Ferdinand.

And who, my lurves, is now @Ferdy.

I create his persona on FB and Insta and TikTok and Twitter. And every other tool of narcissism that is out there. And now I am really getting wet. I even feel my clit tingle as I imagine filming us for my OnlyFans. Oh, the things I would do to have it, to hold it, to make it cum like it has never cummed before!

And then it moves.

Or @Ferdy moves and heads to @Basti who is talking in hushed tones with @Vicente.

The two fuckers stop whispering and before both of them can react, @Ferdy whips out something from his pants and smacks @Basti with it.

Blood is drawn and I see that @Ferdy is holding a gun.

A fucking gun.

But of course.

This is a Friday after all.

Storm? Check.

Cocaine? Check.

Champagne? Check.

The slut? Check.

The retard? Check.

The heartbreaker? Check.

The ghost that is Rafa? Double check.

And now, a loaded gun in the hands of none other than the ghost that is @Ferdy who used to be Rafa?

Check, check, check!!!

Get ready my lurves for some fucking doomscrolling like you have never doomscrolled before.

For the very first time, I see a look of worry painted on the very punchable face of @Vicente.

As if his retarded mind can process what a gun in @Ferdy's hand means.

Meanwhile, the handsome face of @Basti is a canvas of violence and there is pain and anger and hurt, even betrayal. Also, for the very first time, I see that @Basti knows he has lost control of this night, of this fucking summoning, of the unfolding narrative. That this Friday night is no longer his Friday night.

He spits blood and venom as he explains to the retard how @Ferdy got a gun.

And get this, my lurves, it turns out that the loaded gun in @Ferdy's hand was from Familia Gutierrez' small gunrunning biz. The fucking irony.

My iPhone awakens. Pings, alerts, notifications stream in, rivaling the sound and the lightshow courtesy of the tropical storm whipping the metropolis and making this city its beyatch.

As @Pia, that adorable little slut, rubbernecks, I check out the alerts.

O.

M.

G.

"Unreal," I hear myself whisper when I finally find my breathing.

Here's the digits of @Ferdy, my lurves.

41 million comments.

43 million likes.

47 million follower requests and counting.

And these numbers are just on FB alone.

The whole social media scene of the Philippines is being grabbed by @Ferdy by the balls.

Like any—fuck this word—influencer I want in on this.

And to be very clear as fuck to @Pia, I utter my intention aloud.

I'm calling dibs on this @Ferdy.

"Well, with these digits, I am so gonna have him do a version two point oh of my brokenvm hymenvm. My god, that gigantvm penisivm must be so deleeesh!

"Not just once, but maybe twice! Livestreamed on my OnlyFans! Think of the likes! The comments! The hearts! The fucking dollars!"

I update my status on all my socials to "It's Complicated" and end my posts with a broken heart emoji.

And done.

I know, I know. This needs some explaaaaaaaaaaaay.

In the biz, this is called the establishing shot. A preliminary narrative that builds the story arc. Yep, my lurves, a fucking teaser before the big reveal. A foreplay before a proper fuck.

This Friday night is not yet through and there is still a lot of shit that I still have to do.

Chapter Forty-Nine

This is what I do.

"This Friday is over and we should all go home," I say to Mitzi. "The storm seems to have passed and besides, it is already a bit late."

A quiet descends upon the room.

Even the wind is silent.

No thunder, no lightning.

Not a single iPhone vibrates.

Not a single person breathes.

"Rafa?" This is from Mitzi.

"Rafa! Ohhheeemgeee! Is that really you?" This is from Pia.

"Men...I'm glad you're back!" This is from Basti.

"Vicente does not believe this. No, no, no. Not in the fucking least." This is from you know who.

Another round of silence follows.
  It is absolute.
  And alive.
  And carnivorous.
  When this silence starts getting uncomfortable, I laugh.
  A loud and booming laughter that conquers the room and echoes within my mind.

After a second, everyone joins me in the laughter.
  With a collective laugh that is as loud and as long as my laughter.
  And here's the thing.
  The laughter sounds heartfelt.
  Like its coming from a group of very close friends who are having an awesome time hanging out with each other.
  Just like any other Friday night.

If this Friday night is a novel, the very moment after my laughter—*our* laughter—could have been evidence of catharsis being achieved.
  Their emotions seem real.
  Their actions seem real.

Everything seems real.

To quote Pia, "All the feelz, all for realz."

See?

Catharsis.

The hug between Mitzi and Pia.

The fist bump that Basti exchanges with Vicente.

The groufies, with everyone taking turns in taking the shot with two beautiful young women doing air kisses towards the camera.

Basti's kiss, yes, on the mouth and with tongue this time, with Pia.

Mitzi's "Awww..." directed first at the kissing couple, before landing at Vicente who looks away and stares at the rain-slicked window and the darkness beyond.

Mitzi's hug with Vicente.

The girly giggle by Pia after Basti's long passionate kiss.

Basti's handshake and bro hug with Vicente.

These all seem real.

Chapter Fifty

Here's what's fucking real, my lurves.

@Ferdy is going into a hard—and no, I don't mean his gigantvm penisivm, you fucking pervos—reset using obfuscated code to hide his true purpose of canceling us all.

Like a true cultural anthropologist on this cancel culture thingy, he is taking things slow and steady.

And get this, even the fucking weather cooperates.

The storm ceases and all the bells and whistles that came with it also stop.

There is quiet. There is stillness.

@Ferdy turns to me and says these words:

"This Friday is over and we should all go home. The storm seems to have passed and besides, it is already a bit late."

See?

Obfuscated code.

"Rafa?" I say to @Ferdy pretending to be unsuspecting, afraid, affected.

But I am just getting in the game, playing in the reality that @Ferdy is creating, positioning myself as a dependable co-creator in the story that he is spinning.

Yep, my lurves, I can obfuscate my shit, too.

Everyone's buying it.

The adorable little slut @Pia squeals again.

The silly little heartbreaker @Basti welcomes his friend back into the fold.

Except for that retard @Vicente who, in his third person lunacy, does a Cassandra and declares, "Vicente does not believe this. No, no, no. Not in the fucking least."

@Ferdy then laughs.

And what a laughter it is.

Inside the confines of the double-locked penthouse, this laughter summons all the emotions being held by everyone and releases them into the aether.

And this laughter is as loud as it is long.

After all of us recover from this outburst, we all join in this laughter.

We all laugh like we have never laughed before.

And it feels amazeballs.

And it feels awesome.

We all feel that we are alive.

Sweet, sweet release comes like a shared orgasm.

Correct, my lurves.

@Ferdy is a—fuck this word—a fucking influencer.

Because with that one laughter, the following happens.

I hug @Pia.

@Vicente does the fist bump with @Basti.

@Basti kisses @Pia, on the lips, with tongue. Lots of.

@Pia giggles with her cum voice.

@Vicente bro hugs @Basti.

Pics or didn't happen, right my lurves?

And so we all take our selfies and groufies, taking turns in taking the shot, and rearranging ourselves this way and that, all for the perfect shot that would document and immortalize this day before we all conveniently forget it as just another champagne-fueled, cocaine-loaded Friday.

But.

Chapter Fifty-One

But.

But...

But!

Only two things on this stormy Friday night are real.

First. That everyone will forget what happened.

"Let's all just forget about this Friday," I say.

Everyone is in agreement with this idea.

After all the selfies and the groufies, the bro hugs and the fist bumps, the kisses and the embraces, someone actually says, "O. M. G. Yes, let's all just do that. Please."

And the replies are—

"Absolutely!

"Totally!"

Imagine that.

This Friday night is not yet over but everyone thinks that it is for the best that they all forget my dictatorial rule.

And then someone adds, "For realz!"

The second thing that's real?

The gun in my hand.

Oh, fuck yes!

On this dark and stormy Friday night, I am still gripping a fully loaded .22 caliber pistol.

Chapter Fifty-Two

S*o.*
There is a loaded gun in @Ferdy's hand.
And he is going to cancel us all.
Things are getting real weird, real fast that this story, my story, just might not make any sense at all.
Everything is going to get fucked. My narrative structure, my tightly plotted arc, my story design. Even my brand aesthetic, my free spirit persona, the construct that is Marie Celine Gallofin Ricafort that is @Mitzi to all of you my lurves, is in peril. Mortal peril.
Death, IRL, is the final cancellation.
I take another look at the analog killing machine in @Ferdy's hand.
And then I realize that I, too, have my very own weapon.
Right there in my right hand.
A digital killing machine called an iPhone.
And so, I do what I do best.
I cancel someone.
Moi.
When everything is quiet and everyone is holding their breath, I unleash my coup de grâce.

"Mitzi is dead!" I declare as I work my way through all of my socials, updating my profile as I create my latest persona.

I pivot like I have never pivoted before, a reset like I have never reset before, a rebrand like I have never rebranded before.

"Hello @Meldy!"

Correct, my lurves.

Je sui @Meldy.

And no sooner than I have canceled myself when I hear @Ferdy fire the loaded gun.

Chapter Fifty-Three

I fire the gun.

The report is loud as fuck.

And for a split second, a blast of lightning illuminates the entire penthouse in blinding whiteness.

Then absolute blackness comes as thunder descends.

I fire the gun again.

The same deafening shot rings inside the room. And inside my head.

When the light comes back, everything seems darker than before. *Is* darker than before.

The arc lamp, the track lights, even the neon signs out the window are reduced to dying stars.

The darkness that grips every one of us is as patient and as final as the waiting grave.

And so is the stillness.

I say aloud to everyone, to no one.

"I.

"Am.

"The.

"Summoning."

"Men..."

This I hear from Basti. That fucker.

His patented first word, which might very well be his last.

Something that, even if he tries, he can no longer complete into a sentence that would make any sense.

"Now and at the hour of Vicente's death, Amen."

This I hear from who the fuck else but Vicente. That fucktard.

A whimper.

This I hear from Pia. That fuckerette.

She is crying as she stares at the bodies lying bloody on the floor.

Tears streaming down her beautiful face.

Tears that could either be for Basti or for Vicente or maybe even for both of them.

Tears that are as real as the deaths beneath her feet.

I walk over to her.

She slumps down.

I pick her up.

Tilt her head to the blood-splattered corpses.

"See that, Pia?" I whisper.

"That's how you use the word 'literally.' As in: 'Their heads literally exploded.' And no, you don't have to add 'for realz.'"

A gasp.

This I hear from Mitzi.

"@Ferdy," Mitzi whispers.

"We can totally do this once. Maybe twice. Turn plunder and dictatorship and murder into a family business. Yes sir, you and me. Me and you. We can go into politics together. But first, please allow me to update my relationship status.

"In...a...relationship...with...His...Excellency...President...Ferdinand...E...Marcos, Sr, Full deets on my OnlyFans. Subscribe now for only $49.99 a month. Heart emoji. Eggplant emoji. Droplets emoji. Fireworks emoji. Done!"

Mitzi shows me her iPhone as she smiles the sweetest smile I have ever witnessed.

See?

What did I tell you about Mitzi having balls?

I look at her.

I wait for her to say "Rafa?"

Yes, a name that is both a command and a promise.

It does not come.

What she does is open the camera on her iPhone.

"This needs to be filmed, my lurve," Mitzi says as she unzips my pants and fondles my Presidential erection.

She takes her time in working my *membrvm virilvm*, getting everything into the frame.

And then she asks me: "Whose gigantic dick is this? This could not be yours!"

I reply with: "That dick belongs to Ferdinand Emmanuel Edralin Marcos, Sr.!"

She takes my *gigantvm penisivm* inside her mouth.

I let out a moan as I will my knees to keep me vertical.

Oh, my beautiful Meldy, my one and only Meldy, this free spirit whose gorgeous mouth is the window into her very own soul.

She locks her eyes into mine.

"Cum for me, Ferdinand, cum for me, baby, cum for your dear Meldy," Mitzi purrs.

And that, right there, with my Presidential penis inside Mitzi's mouth, she resurrects the dead language that I have uttered into a romance language.

Ever so slowly she edges me for a moment, for an eternity, teasing me, tormenting me.

And with one masterstroke involving her tongue and her cheeks with just the right amount of teeth, such sweet release comes.

Ohmyfuckinggods.

I shudder and restore myself from my little death, pulling my glistening erection off her wet and glistening lips.

Mitzi smiles and uses her fingers to lick a few drops of my Presidential spermatozoa from her lower lip. As a finale for her little movie, she swallows, blows an air kiss to the camera, and winks.

I holster my Presidential penis inside my boxers, zip up my pants.

I listen to the silence that follows.

Have you ever done that, listen to the silence in your head?

It's a very enlightening experience, believe you me.

Just listen.

Disregard all the shit in there. The porn. The drugs and the alcohol. The posts and the likes and the shares and the hearts.

The fears. The regrets. Whatever crap that is in there, drowning you, deafening you.

Really listen.

You can hear your innermost thoughts with a kind of clarity you wouldn't have thought possible. And if you try hard enough, you can even hear the future.

That Friday night, I listen to the silence. And it's telling me that great things are happening.

I am starting my own family business.

I am going into politics.

With my BAE Mitzi, the very same Mitzi who is now @Meldy.

@Ferdy and @Meldy sounds perfect.

As I listen to the silence, I can also feel something.

That I am in the moment.

That I am in the present.

And I finally find my peace.

Chapter Fifty-Four

T take my peace wherever I can find it.

From my snow, from my moolah, from my porn.

Especially from my porn.

For I always achieve la petit mort every time I do myself for my OnlyFans.

Swear to gods, hope to die.

I cum every time I am on cam. That's the performance of my life. That's the story of my life.

But on this Friday night, what gets me off is a different kind of porn.

The best kind of porn.

Revenge porn.

I know, I know.

I am just an active participant as it is @Rafa who does most of the revenging in this story, my story, but think of what I am telling you now, my lurves, as a dark post, a curated content specifically targeted to you. I know you all can keep a dirty little secret.

@Ferdy fires the gun.

Once.

Twice.

The sound is maddening, deafening that it rivals the thunder from the heavens and in perfect cadence with the gunfire comes total darkness, the room, illuminated only by the lightning that follows.

Yep, my lurves, the storm is not yet done but has just made a turn, a pivot if you will, as it redoubles its assault.

When the power comes back on, @Basti and @Vicente are on the floor, both of them muttering something inconsequential while they surrender to the pull of gradual irrelevance as they drown in their own respective pools of blood. Talk about an immersive experience.

I know, I know, but I just couldn't resist.

The sight is so deleeesh.

@Basti, the leet is having his own end-of-life moment like a discarded software no longer supported by the manufacturer.

@Vicente, he who speaks in the third, is getting murdered in the third.

Double murder, double deleeesh.

And then @Ferdy breaks the silence as he declares his very being.

With just four words, he asserts that he is the proto-influencer.

I stand corrected, my lurves.

@Ferdy is the ur-influencer.

And this is what @Ferdy utters:

"I.

"Am.

"The.

"Summoning!"

I gasp as I hear these words.

I do something I have never done before.

I do my own math where the value of X equals life.

I do a collab.

@Ferdy X @Meldy.

I open my iPhone.

I pose and take a couple of photos with @Ferdy.

I do the edits and choose the best one, the one with moi *favoring the cam.*

I update my relationship status as I upload this photo of my meet-cute, my boyfriend reveal, my fan selfie day all rolled into one post.

"In a relationship with His Excellency President Ferdinand E. Marcos, Sr. Full deeets on my OnlyFans. Subscribe now for only $49.99 a month."

And just to be on brand, I add the heart, the eggplant, the droplets, and the fireworks emojis.

I show my status to @Ferdy, my @Ferdy.

He approves.

I screenshot this status and save it.

For the future.

This will be my very own NFT that will sell to the highest bidder. Surely, it will rake in the moolah in the form of Bitcoin. Benjamins, even crisp ones, are so yesterday.

While @Pia, that adorable little slut, watches, I open the camera app, click on video, and start filming.

I unzip @Ferdy's jeans and say hello to his gigantvm penisivm, *taking it in my left hand, stroking it, fondling it, squeezing it.*

I even do our inside joke, asking him whose gigantic dick I am holding.

The reply, as I have expected, is that it belongs to Ferdinand Emmanuel Edralin Marcos, Sr.

@Ferdy sighs as I take it all in my waiting mouth, inch by inch until I have his whole membrvm virilvm *inside of me.*

I take my time, teasing @Ferdy until I sense that he just can't take it anymore and then I unleash the Kraken that is my tongue and the sides of my cheeks and the depth of my throat. I let my whole mouth work its magic the way I have learned it from the finishing school in Switzerland. Who says getting an education will not save you?

And then, making sure that everything is inside the frame and observing the rule of thirds, I deploy my highly curated words as I do my highly calibrated teeth.

No, not that "Rafa?" that is both a command and a promise.

I command @Ferdy like I have never commanded him before as I ever so slowly graze the head of his peen with my perfectly awesome teeth.

"Cum for me, Ferdinand, cum for me, baby, cum for your dear Meldy."

And guess what, my lurves?

I also cum like I have never cummed before.

@Ferdy sighs and shudders and showers me with his lurve and I do my best not to let a single drop go to waste. I swallow like a good Catholic schoolgirl and lick any wayward drop off my lower lip.

I blow a kiss to the camera before saving my masterpiece, this once-in-a-lifetime bukkake captured in the glory of bokeh.

After double-checking that the vid has been saved into the iCloud, I take the loaded gun from @Ferdy's hand.

I turn to @Pia, who has been watching us all this while, her face full of envy. On her face is not some low-grade envy but the Biblical "Thou Shalt Not Covet Thy Neighbor's Husband" level of FOMO. The adorable little slut has been reduced to that of a spectator, a voyeur, a non-participant in an event that will soon trend. That will soon go viral, like no other vid has gone viral before.

And she has all the right to this envy for I know that the last time @Pia went viral was when her vag got a yeast infection from getting dicked by some randos ordered from the internet.

Anyhoo.

I aim the pistol square into @Pia's forehead.

Point and shot, just like the iPhone's camera.

I squeeze the trigger of this analog killing machine that has no need for an OS update to do its awesome job.

And just like that, I slay the adorable little slut.

The report and the recoil come simultaneously.

Bone and blood and brain matter erupt from her skull as, yep, I just couldn't resist, her head literally exploded.

For realz.

And then a waft of sulfur comes, as intoxicating as the snow I have inhaled earlier.

Everything inside my head settles. Like all the stars in the universe have just aligned. And that order has been restored.

Correct, my lurves. I have a very positive outlook in life that I need not mine history for fresh outrage so that I can find the courage to cancel someone. Yep, I may be broke as fuck but I don't have an overdraft in my righteous indignation account that would negate any aggression withdrawal I would like to do.

As @Pia spasms on the floor, I bend over and look her in the eyes just before they freeze and turn to glass.

"The question, my lurve, is not 'How's Life?' but 'How's death?' You fucking jologette."

I know, I know.

I haven't forgotten that one secret in the influencing biz.

That one lesson that you all need to learn from this story, my story.

Take a safety shot.

Always.

And so, I empty the remaining bullets on the three bodies lying still on the bloody floor.

I do another sign of the inverted cross as I utter an inverse of my favorite quote from the Book of Revelations.

"And in those days shall men not seek death, but still shall find it; and shall desire not to die, but death shall run unto them."

And just like that, @Basti the silly little heartbreaker, @Pia the adorable little slut, and @Vicente the lousy little retard are all canceled like they are just three of the trillions of ephemeral content floating in the aether that have just been deleted.

THE FUCKING END

Epilogue

A nd this is how our story ends.

Shit did happen on this stormy Friday night.

And that climax. That explosive climax. Literally and figuratively, amirite?

As promised, there are no lessons to be learned.

That would be pretentious. To expect a moral from this particular story. Stupid even.

Because really, as the saying goes: the more it changes, the more it stays the same.

But if you think otherwise, it is time to FB and tweet and TikTok and snap and 'gram this shit.

And, of course, discuss.

And so, my lurves, we come to the end of this story.

My story.

In an ending that is trending like no other trend has trended before. Awesomeness.

And of course, that lesson!

Because what would be the point, if you, my lurves, all learn nothing from moi? That would be a shame.

Because as I always keep saying: plus ça change, plus c'est la même chose.

So now I am giving you, my lurves, the chance to share or heart or quote my story.

Don't forget to @ me.

Acknowledgments

Manuscripts don't burn but neither do they leap from my laptop to your hands.

I am very grateful to Christoph Paul of CLASH BOOKS who got the story and whose enthusiasm made the book that it is today.

This enthusiasm is shared by the rest of the CLASH BOOKS crew and they deserve a full salute: Leza Cantoral, Kaitlyn Kessinger, Miloh Elena Gorgevska, and Matthew Revert.

Salamat to Jose Dalisay Jr., a writer's writer, for his direction that I head over to the analog repository of the dictator's proclamations and delusions, speeches and lunacies that is The Philippine National Library.

Salamat to Eileen Tabios, champion of underrepresented writers, for her tireless promotion of our publications in the digital realm.

Salamat to Dean and Nikki Alfar, editors extraordinaire, for their works that continue to inspire me as a writer of speculative fiction.

Cheers to my friends here in the United States and around the world: Ellen Myra Sy, Emily Aquino, Bobwen Tampus, Forrest Harrison Gerke, Matie and Mike Maraño, Bambi and Alvin Camano, Shellah and Javier Gomez, JLo and Jay Sembrano, Rochelle and Keith Donoghue, Che and Jonathan Dalmasi, Pris and Joel Francisco, Meac and Mong San Gabriel, Bambi and Richie Breganza, Mel and Paul Rocco, Grace and Damon Rogers, Verna Quinton, Kenneth

Inocencio, Osang and Ritchie Arceo, Ning and Nold Villania, Joel Zubeldia, Bujit and Jake Tesoro, V-Ann and Donny Dingcong, Maia Joven, Bhavna Thakur, Dante Dizon, Je de Asas, Angie Tijam-Tohid, and Julio Malantic.

Salud to the founding members of *Tomadors Without Borders*: Allan Sindo, EJ Jaingue, Jojo Jaingue, and Arvi Jaingue.

And as always, I am forever thankful to Joy, my lurve.

About the Author

Photo by Benjamin Chan / Blacksheep Photography

Jose Elvin Bueno is a first-generation immigrant to the United States from the Philippines. He is a fictionist, playwright, and novelist. His debut novel *Subversivo, Inc.* is the recipient of the Grand Prize in the 63rd Palanca Awards for Literature, the Philippines' most prestigious literary prize. He is also the author of the novel *Sindicato & Co.*

He lives in New York where he is writing his next book.

Also by CLASH Books

STRANGE STONES

Edward Lee & Mary SanGiovanni

THE PINK AGAVE MOTEL

V. Castro

THE BODY HARVEST

Michael J. Seidlinger

EVERYTHING THE DARKNESS EATS

Eric LaRocca

FLOWERS FROM THE VOID

Gianni Washington

LETTERS TO THE PURPLE SATIN KILLER

Joshua Chaplinsky

THE KING OF VIDEO POKER

Paolo Iacovelli

SELENE SHADE: RESURRECTIONIST FOR HIRE

Victoria Dalpe

INVAGINIES

Joe Koch

THE BLACK TREE ATOP THE HILL

Karla Yvette

WE PUT THE LIT IN LITERARY

CLASHBOOKS.COM

FOLLOW US

IG

X

FB

@clashbooks